THE FALL GUY

THE FALL GUY

RITCHIE PERRY

A MIDNIGHT NOVEL OF SUSPENSE

HOUGHTON MIFFLIN COMPANY BOSTON

1972

PROLOGUE

CHARLES PAWSON sat at the desk in his office off Queen Victoria Street, paying more attention to the rumble of the London rush-hour traffic outside than to the pile of reports in front of him. As head of SR(2) his life alternated between periods of hectic activity, when the resources of the department were stretched to their limit, and periods of drab routine, as mundane as in any branch of the Establishment. For the moment business was slack, something which accounted for Pawson's boredom. The SR in the department's title stood for Special Responsibilities, while the numeral had become a meaningless appendage, merely serving to eliminate any chance of confusion with a popular brand of toothpaste. Originally, when a late, little-lamented Home Secretary had had his brainwave, there had been an SR(1) section as well, but this had been a short-lived experiment, soon being swallowed and digested by Pawson's predecessor. Now SR(2) stood alone, basically an adjunct to the police, operating where Special Branch, Interpol and other more regularly constituted forces were unable to go. Pawson was responsible only to the Minister and his brief wasn't to amass evidence for the benefit of judge and jury. It was to cut out cancers which had refused to respond to less drastic treatment. In his morbid moments Pawson saw himself as the successor to Pierrepoint, only, instead of a rope, he used the SR(2) operatives, a not so select band of highly trained assassins. In his more cheerful moods he admitted that this was only a small part of the picture, that the department played a not insignificant role in national security, but usually he gave the matter no thought at all. He had been given a job to do and this he did to the best of his ability.

For the time being he was simply bored and the prospect of a visit from Superintendent Davies, a member of

5

the Drug Squad at Scotland Yard, did nothing to brighten his day. He had no need for a crystal ball to guess what the visit presaged and, initially, he'd been tempted to fob off the superintendent with some excuse about overwork. Then other considerations had combined to change his mind, not least among them being his uncomfortable awareness of the impending annual appropriations review. With the grisly memory of the Czech Trade Mission still to be eradicated, it was the time of year to rake in all possible kudos.

The reports pushed to one side, Pawson glanced at his watch, swearing under his breath when he saw his visitor was overdue. Restless, he crossed to the window to shoo away the pigeons which were the bane of his life, wrinkling his nose in disgust at the white droppings on the sill. Five minutes later he was still standing there, gazing down at the people in the street, when the intercom buzzed. Unhurriedly he returned to his desk.

'Superintendent Davies has arrived, sir,' his secretary informed him.

'About time,' Pawson commented sourly. 'Give me a couple of minutes, then send him through.'

Sitting down, Pawson switched on the small tape-recorder concealed in the top drawer of his desk, a precaution he employed with every caller but one he considered especially necessary in his dealings with the police. Years of experience had taught him they were almost as devious as politicians. When his secretary ushered in the superintendent Pawson was puffing at his pipe and he used the smoke to screen his swift appraisal of the policeman, a tall, raw-boned man in his forties with a shock of carrot-red hair. Without rising to his feet, Pawson motioned him to a seat on the far side of the desk. He was a firm believer in establishing authority from the very start.

'Well, Davies,' he said brusquely. 'What dirty work have you brought me this time? I suppose your boys have made

6

some horrible balls-up and you expect me to clear up after you.'

The approach was one which seldom failed to work with policemen and, to Pawson's considerable amusement, the superintendent's face reddened. Going cap in hand to the head of SR(2) was not a task for which senior police officers competed.

'It isn't like that at all, sir,' Davies protested, visibly restraining himself. 'We've a case on our hands at the moment which we feel is more in your line of country. That's all.'

Pawson's smile wasn't designed to smooth ruffled feathers.

'What a beautiful euphemism,' he murmured. 'Do elucidate.'

'It's the cocaine business,' Davies persisted doggedly, doing his best to ignore the sarcasm. 'We'd like you to take over the foreign end of the investigation. We'll attend to the distributors here in the United Kingdom.'

Pawson swivelled round in his chair so he could look out of the window at the shorthand-typists in the office block across the street.

'I see,' he said, his back half turned to Davies. 'What progress have you made so far?'

'Not a great deal,' Davies was forced to admit. 'We've made several arrests but they've all been small fry. Pushers and middlemen.'

Turning back to him, Pawson picked up a pencil and examined the point. He was finding the interview far more diverting than he'd anticipated.

'How about the other end?' he asked, keeping his eyes on the pencil. 'Do you know where the cocaine is coming from? Or how it's being brought into the country?'

'Not really,' Davies answered, flushing again. 'We know the source is in South America and we're positive the cocaine is coming into Britain by ship but that's all. I appreciate it isn't a great deal of information to work on but . . .'

7

Davies shrugged his shoulders helplessly.

'Surely Interpol or local police forces must have turned up with more than that?'

'Interpol has its limits,' the superintendent said, speaking with more confidence now he was back on safer ground, 'and South America is one of them. To operate really efficiently it relies on well organized, co-operative national police forces. South of the United States border they're in extremely short supply. In fact there's so much bribery and palm greasing nearly all the forces are corrupt from top to bottom. The men behind the cocaine smuggling are operating on a large scale, so large they're bound to have plenty of police connections. They'd almost certainly learn of any move against them through the local police before it had a chance to leave the ground. That's no good to us. We're not interested in stopping the traffic for a few weeks. We want it completely disrupted, otherwise the whole operation is pointless. If possible we'd like SR(2) to roll up the entire organization, all the way from the source of supply to the port of embarkation. Once that's done the problem over here virtually disappears.'

A thin smile appeared on Pawson's face, a danger signal to anyone who knew him well. He stopped toying with the pencil, for the first time looking the policeman straight in the eye.

'In other words you're asking me to undertake illegal activities on foreign soil,' he queried coldly.

'You're phrasing the proposition very harshly,' Davies blustered, taken aback by the new line of attack. 'Surely nearly every mission you undertake abroad is technically illegal.'

'I'm not denying the fact,' Pawson said glacially, inwardly delighted by Davies's alacrity in rising to the bait. 'I was merely trying to fathom police mentality. You actively encourage interference in territories abroad but when you unearth similar activity in this country you scream blue, bloody murder. I can just imagine the Yard's reaction if it was by-passed by a foreign law enforcement agency. By the FBI, say. It was bad enough when one of my men borrowed a member of that Czech trade delegation for a few hours.'

In Pawson's profession it was criminal negligence not to kick an opponent when he was down. Davies wasn't exactly an opponent but Pawson intended to kick him just the same.

'Anyway,' he continued, when Davies offered no defence, 'I'm prepared to do as you ask, although I naturally can't guarantee results. There is one condition, though.' Pawson paused for effect, allowing Davies to wince in anticipation. 'I not only want complete, independent control of the foreign end of the operation, I must also insist that the police make no move in this country without my prior authorization. There has to be a co-ordinator and I intend to make it my job, not Scotland Yard's.'

Having delivered his ultimatum Pawson sat back and watched the superintendent's evident discomfiture with cynical detachment. Try as he might Davies couldn't conceal his confusion and resentment.

'I don't know about that, sir,' he objected. 'It is primarily a police matter.'

'If you remember, this was precisely the point I was endeavouring to make earlier,' Pawson said sweetly. 'I'm afraid it's the price you'll have to pay for my co-operation. In fact until your superiors agree to meet my request, I refuse to commit a single one of my agents. I don't want the right hand not knowing what the left is doing and in this partnership SR(2) will definitely be the right hand.'

The air-conditioning was out of order and they were lying with the sheet thrown back, their bodies well apart. Mary was asleep, tendrils of blonde hair sticking damply to her forehead, one hand cupped chastely over her groin. Enviously Reece wondered how the hell she managed to sleep in the almost insufferable heat. It was just his luck she had to live in Belem, not in Rio, Sao Paulo, Montevideo or even Buenos Aires, somewhere civilized instead of a festering port at the mouth of the Amazon. He was the only permanent SR(2) agent south of the Amazon and east of the Andes, with literally millions of women to choose from, yet he'd had to plump for an Englishwoman living in one of the most uncomfortable cities in the Americas. And she was married. Reece was brooding about this, wondering where he'd made his mistake, when the telephone beside the bed rang. Drowsily he lifted the receiver.

'There's a call from London for you,' the hotel telephonist told him.

Nervously Reece glanced at Mary, who was still asleep beside him, apparently undisturbed by the noise.

'Hold the line for me,' he said quickly. 'I'll take the call downstairs.'

Hastily he pulled on his shirt and trousers before slipping out of the room. To Reece's mind the call could only mean trouble. Pawson was the one person who knew where to contact him and this was the first occasion in three years that he'd resorted to direct communication. There was an anxious five minutes' wait, then Pawson was put through.

'I'm beginning to think you must have a fancy woman in Belem,' Pawson said by way if introduction. 'This makes your fifth visit in the last six months.'

'I don't come here from choice, sir,' Reece responded, not wholly untruthfully. 'It's all in my reports.'

'I know. That's why I'm wasting the taxpayers' money by phoning you. The Brazilian cocaine trade is hardly our line of country.'

The conversation had already taken a nasty turn, making Reece sweat far more than the temperature warranted. He'd known his repeated trips to see Mary were a mistake but he'd thought he'd covered his tracks rather neatly. Now he knew better. A written reprimand would have meant nothing, a personal phone call from Pawson quite possibly meant the end of his attachment to SR(2).

'I disagree, sir,' he protested, more than a hint of desperation behind the words. 'When you posted me here you told me South America was a backwater. You said the only way to justify my presence here was to use my intuition, to investigate things which weren't of obvious interest to the department but which I felt might have some significance. That's exactly what I've been doing here in Belem.'

Reece stopped, aware that he might just as well have admitted that he came to Belem to see Mary. Even to his own ears the story had sounded painfully thin.

'Excuse me for being obtuse,' Pawson said, not making things any easier, 'but perhaps you'd care to explain the significance to me.'

Reece took a deep breath and marshalled his thoughts.

'Until recently,' he began, 'nearly all the cocaine reaching the eastern seaboard of the United States was shipped out through Belem. The coca leaves grew, and still grew in the foothills of the Andes. They were roughly processed on the spot, then shipped down the Amazon and out through Belem. Naturally the Americans objected to this and they've put increasing pressure on the Brazilian authorities to take some action. As a result the cocaine traffic has reduced to a trickle, both out of Belem and into the States. This interested me because it stood to reason that the cocaine must be going somewhere else. The coca leaves grow wild and don't need any cultivation, the processing is relatively simple compared with heroin and the profits are fantastic. If the cocaine wasn't being sent to the States the obvious alternative market was western Europe, including Britain. I started my investigation to find out whether my suspicions were correct.'

'And were they?' Pawson prompted. 'Is there anything you can add to your last report?'

'I'm afraid not,' Reece admitted unhappily. 'All I've learned is that the coca leaves are being flown out to the south now instead of going down the Amazon by boat.'

There was a silence, a silence costing God knew how many pounds a second. With the receiver clutched clammily in his hand Reece waited for the axe to fall and Pawson's next words took him completely by surprise.

'Luckily for you your suspicions were correct,' he said. 'The cocaine is coming into Britain in large quantities.' Pawson paused. 'The trade has to be stopped. You're to return to base in Sao Paulo and be ready for further instructions. Meanwhile I'm activating all observers. Once I know where the coca leaves are being flown to you're in business. It's high time you started earning your salary.'

Among the men who received Pawson's memorandum from London was one called Jim Peters, although to everyone in Porto Alegre he was known as Otto Schmidt, owner of the Scheherazade restaurant. Short, squat and unprepossessing, his swarthy complexion and Zapata moustache gave him the appearance of an English stage spy. In Brazil they meant he could pass unnoticed where other north Europeans were singled out immediately. By rights he should have had an administrative post in London and it had been his own choice to enter semi-retirement in Porto Alegre. He was a man with an obsession. During the war, although not a Jew himself, he had infiltrated one of the Polish concentration camps, helping to organize escape routes and collecting evidence against the German officers in charge. In the line of duty he had lived the life of a Jewish prisoner, never knowing whether the next day would be his last. He emerged, after the Russian liberation of the camp, several stones lighter in weight and possessed of a loathing for the Nazis no Jew could match. For the next three years he had worked in West Germany tracking down fugitive war criminals, unrivalled in his dedication. When Pawson's predecessor had suggested a transfer to London Peters had refused point-blank, saying he intended to settle in one of the regions of South America where the major ex-Nazis were thought to have fled. Even now, twenty-five years after the end of hostilities, he retained close links with Israeli intelligence as well as with SR(2) and had played a minor role in the capture of Eichmann. Pawson was fully aware of the connection and raised no objections. Even if Peters was seldom called upon, his experience as an agent made him too valuable an observer to lose.

Peters read through the memorandum in his office at the rear of the restaurant, only half-aware of the clatter of pans and sizzling of fat in the kitchen next door. He'd been in the business far too long to need a code book in order to decipher the directive. When he'd finished reading, the instructions fully absorbed, he slumped back in his chair, thinking hard. In the twenty-odd years that Porto Alegre had been his home Peters had cultivated a wide range of acquaintances and something a fellow restaurateur had let slip a few weeks previously nagged at his memory. For several minutes he debated whether or not there could possibly be a link with the subject of Pawson's concern. He didn't want to raise a false alarm, yet at the same time it would be negligent of him not to follow up the information. In the end Peters decided on a compromise. Pulling a notepad towards him he wrote: 'RE YOUR TELEX HAVE POSSIBLE LEAD STOP TRAVELLING TO RIO GRANDE TOMORROW STOP FULLER REPORT WILL FOLLOW SCHMIDT.' Working faster now the decision was made, he coded the message on to a telegram blank, addressing it to a small import-export company in Sao Paulo. From there it would be telexed to SR(2) headquarters in London.

As Peters entered the room Biddencourt rose from behind the desk, extending his hand in greeting.

'Otto!' he exclaimed. 'What brings you to Rio Grande? I didn't expect to see you for at least another fortnight.'

'I had other business down here so I thought I'd kill two birds with one stone,' Peters explained, sinking into a seat. 'I don't like this god-forsaken hole enough to come here more often than's absolutely necessary.'

For half an hour the two men talked business, calculating the amounts of fish likely to be required at the Scheherazade during the following weeks. On the point of leaving, as an apparent afterthought, Peters asked if he could use Biddencourt's phone. It was a simple task to transfer the tiny, magnetic microphone-cum-transmitter from the palm of his hand to the base of the telephone.

The bug escaped detection for less than an hour, although its discovery was completely fortuitous. Biddencourt was returning an account to the filing cabinet when he banged awkwardly into the corner of the desk, dislodging the telephone in the process. It was as he bent to retrieve the instrument from where it dangled by the flex that he noticed the disc adhering to the base. To the best of his knowledge he had never seen such a device before, but he instantly recognized it for what it was. His initial impulse was to tear it off, then, almost immediately, he realized this would be a mistake. Now that its existence was known the bug no longer posed a threat, whereas removing it would only serve to alert whoever was listening in at the other end. The first priority was to establish the identity of the electronic eavesdropper and discover why he was so interested in Biddencourt's affairs. The police were in no way responsible, of this Biddencourt was sure. He had two reliable men planted at local headquarters, ideally situated to provide ample warning of any move against him. This narrowed the field to people who'd recently had access to the office, and of these Otto Schmidt had been the only one to use the telephone.

Back at his hotel Peters spent a boring, unproductive afternoon monitoring the events in Biddencourt's office. Nothing he overheard was in the least way compromising, and, more and more, he regretted the impulse which had brought him to Rio Grande. He'd known Biddencourt for nearly ten years and, in his personal dealings, there had never been a hint of suspicion. All he had to go on was a casual remark, a half-drunken observation that Biddencourt used fish wholesaling as a front for other, less legal enterprises. In itself this meant nothing. Nearly every Brazilian businessman worth his salt had something going for him and there was no earthly reason why Biddencourt should be an exception.

Nevertheless there was no point in half measures. Once Peters had started to investigate Biddencourt he was duty bound to carry through to a conclusion, positive or otherwise. In his telegram he'd hinted he might be on to something and he had far too much professional pride to file a negative report before he was absolutely certain. In view of the limited time at his disposal the bug had always been a long shot, now more direct methods were called for. Biddencourt's office and house were the obvious targets, but, before he tackled either, Peters intended to have as good a meal as Rio Grande could provide. Like all successful restaurant proprietors, he didn't believe in working on an empty stomach.

Lutz and Joao followed Schmidt when he left his hotel for the nearby Hong Kong restaurant. Joao, the shorter of the two men, went in behind him, Lutz waited outside until Schmidt had ordered his meal before making his unhurried way back to the hotel. He knew exactly what he was looking for and it took him less than five minutes in Schmidt's room to find the receiver. A quarter of an hour later he was phoning Biddencourt from the bar next door to the hotel.

'You can call off the rest of the boys,' Lutz announced as soon as his call was answered. 'Schmidt is the man we want all right.'

'You found the receiver?'

'That's right. It was inside his suitcase.'

'Good. Where are you now?'

'Next door to the hotel,' Lutz told him. 'Schmidt's having dinner at the Hong Kong. Do you want me to join Joao at the restaurant or to wait for him here?'

'That rather depends,' Biddencourt answered slowly. 'What's Schmidt been doing since he left me this morning?'

'Nothing much. He had lunch, then came straight back to the hotel. Until he went out half an hour ago he'd been in his room all the while.'

'Any contacts?'

'None, and he hasn't put any calls through the hotel switchboard. I checked.'

'In that case you can join Joao,' Biddencourt decided after a moment's hesitation. 'Allow Schmidt plenty of rope, don't pick him up unless it's absolutely necessary. First of all I want to know exactly what his game is.'

At midnight Peters was quietly humming the Eton boating song to himself as he sculled gently along the quayside in a borrowed rowing-boat. He was too long in the tooth to fancy clambering over a twelve-foot-high fence with barbed wire on the top if there was a way round. Level with Biddencourt's warehouse he redoubled his efforts to be quiet, scarcely using the oars as he drifted in between the two fishing-boats tied to the wharf. Holding on to a bollard with one hand, he carefully scanned the yard, his head only just above the level of the quay. At first he could see nothing apart from the eerie bulk of the warehouse and the stinking stacks of fish boxes. It was fully ten minutes before his patience was rewarded, a sudden flare of light as the night watchman struck a match. Quickly Peters wound the painter round the bollard, lifted himself on to the quay and scuttled into the shelter of the nearest stack of boxes, his rubber soles making no sound on the cobbles.

Moving towards his objective was a chancy business. At every step he risked standing on one of the horde of cats infesting the yard or stumbling over a loose box and it was a quarter of an hour before he'd worked his way behind the watchman. As a protector of property the man was a dead loss. The first he knew of an intruder was when Peters's thumbs dug into his carotid arteries and by then the knowledge was no longer of any value.

With the watchman safely trussed up Peters had no further need for caution, making directly for the office. The door posed no problems. It was secured by a simple spring lock and, using the thin strip of plastic he'd brought with him, Peters was inside faster than if he'd had the key. Once the lights were on he settled down to work, starting with the filing cabinet and going on to the desk, neither of them yielding anything of interest. The safe was a neat job, set flush in the floor beneath the desk, with only the break in the wall to wall carpet to reveal its existence. Considering the trouble Biddencourt had gone to in concealing the safe Peters was pleasantly surprised to find a combination lock, one of a type he'd been weaned on years before, and the contents amply repaid the time he spent in opening it. Fifty thousand dollars in American currency didn't necessarily mean a thing, although this was an awful lot of ready cash for a fish wholesaler to have in his possession. The bundle of shipping documents, covering coffee exports from Santos to Liverpool, was far more interesting. Of course they could indicate Biddencourt was genuinely involved in the coffee business, but, as a practising sceptic, Peters would have been prepared to wager a year's income that they pertained to a far more lucrative trade. In a legitimate enterprise Biddencourt would have had no need for an assumed name.

Working slowly and methodically, Peters used a whole roll of film in his miniature camera before he replaced the papers. The safe closed, the bug removed from the base of the telephone, Peters prepared to leave, knowing his part was over. Now it was up to Pawson to check in Liverpool; and if cocaine was being smuggled among the coffee beans, a field agent would be sent to Rio Grande. He, Peters, could go back to being a restaurant proprietor pure and simple. Until the next time Pawson needed his services, that is.

Lutz and Joao were waiting for Schmidt when he came out. As Schmidt closed the office door behind him, Lutz, who was standing some twenty yards away, flipped on the warehouse lights. For a man of his age Schmidt reacted surprisingly fast. The unexpected illumination stopped him in his tracks for only a fraction of a second, then he was running hard for the protection of the stacked boxes, bearing to his right, away from Lutz and towards his boat.

It took Peters less than a minute to realize he had no hope of escape. The piles of boxes were of uneven height, some reaching almost to the roof while others stood no more than ten feet from the floor, but the overall layout was on strict geometric lines, the network of corridors between the stacks designed like a grid and crossing each other at right angles. The moment Peters saw the second man at the first intersection he knew he was being played with. He was unarmed, something the opposition must have made sure of beforehand, otherwise they would have taken him directly he left the office. As it was, the men were positioned one on either side, travelling parallel to him and showing no immediate inclination to move in. Their ploy was simple enough and Peters stopped running, saving his breath for later when he'd need it. His situation was comparable to the most basic of chess end games, only, if it had been chess, Peters would have had no hesitation in capitulating. The men were leapfrogging one another so that he was constantly screened, keeping him headed in the direction they wanted and remaining far enough away to make a sudden attack on either of them out of the question. In a very short time he would be forced to the edge of the board, or rather to the edge of the area covered with fish boxes. This was when the real action would start.

At the last line of boxes Peters stopped, temporarily out of sight of his pursuers. The forty-five yards of completely open ground which separated him from the boat looked singularly uninviting. Not that the boat played any further part in his plans. He would have to swim to safety if he made it to the water, and this was a very big if. Peters suspected he'd been allowed as far as his present position merely to provide the other two with some target practice, the light from the warehouse ideal for their purposes.

Nevertheless he was committed. The only alternative was surrender and Peters had few illusions about what this would probably entail.

They were better than he'd expected, far, far better. He went out fast, zigzagging and heading in the least likely direction, away from the boat. Peters had hoped to cover twenty yards before they started shooting, in fact he managed just six strides and they didn't even have to use their guns. Instead the bolas wrapped themselves around his ankles and he crashed down, hitting the slimy cobbles hard. Surprisingly, there was no sound of approaching footsteps. Cautiously Peters sat up to see what the two men were doing, only to discover the answer was nothing. They were standing in the shadows, making no move towards him. Evidently the game wasn't yet over.

The fact he knew it was only a game, albeit a deadly game he had no hope of winning, didn't alter Peters's determination. To give in would be senseless, especially as he now possessed a weapon of sorts. Slowly he unravelled the bolas, rubbing his bruised ankles before he rose to his feet. It was still thirty-five yards to the water.

'Start running,' the smaller of the two called to him. 'We're getting bored.'

No general could hope to retain his command if he was tortured with guilt every time one of his soldiers was killed, and, in his own peculiar way, Pawson was a general. Agents were killed every now and again, it was one of the facts of life, something which had to be accepted. Everyone who worked for SR(2) was fully aware of the dangers inherent in the job, while Pawson made it perfectly clear that he had no intention of shedding crocodile tears over anyone who landed himself in trouble. He himself had gleaned the knowledge at an early age, before the present department had been created, being barely twenty-two when he was caught working behind the Japanese lines in China. Although England and Japan were still some years away from war Pawson had been treated, with every reason, as an enemy spy. Only one thing had saved him from a firing squad. For three long months, months from which he still bore the scars, Pawson had refused to break under the most rigorous Japanese interrogation. His subsequent escape had entailed a hazardous trek lasting another two months, his own efforts to reach safety repeatedly nullified by the speed of the Japanese advance. When he was eventually invalided out of Hong Kong and back to London, Pawson had expected a hero's return. Instead he'd been comprehensively debriefed, reprimanded for his stupidity in falling into Japanese hands and subjected to a barrage of gripes about the length of his convalescence at such an inopportune time. There had been no mention at all of his bravery in the face of torture. It had been a harsh lesson, but one well worth learning.

Consequently Pawson's dominant emotion wasn't pity or even sadness, it was a black, murderous rage, a presence which filled the whole building with misgiving. He'd been thwarted in his hopes of bringing the affair to a speedy conclusion and there was a sense of personal affront at losing even an observer in such a pipsqueak operation. Pawson didn't need to see the body to know Peters must be dead—there was only one way a man of his experience could be kept incommunicado for over a week.

The third and final factor contributing to Pawson's anger was directed at Peters himself, at his failure to pass back any worthwhile information. Of all the observers activated, Peters had been the only one to come up with anything approaching a positive response, his disappearance proving the odds on his line of enquiry being the correct one. All Pawson knew was that Peters had gone to Rio Grande, a city of some 75,000 inhabitants, and Peters had given no indication as to which particular citizen he'd been interested in.

'The bloody idiot,' Pawson snapped, hands clenched deep in his pockets as he stared out of the window. 'How the hell did he expect anyone to follow him up?'

'Perhaps he didn't think he'd run into any trouble.'

No sooner were the words out of his mouth than Reece regretted releasing them. He was dog-tired after the long flight from Sao Paulo, and the change of time zones and the seventy degree drop in temperature, plus God knew how many hours without proper sleep, were hardly designed to have him at the top of his form.

'What did you say?' Pawson demanded, swinging round to glower at him.

Reece clamped his lips firmly together and kept quiet, shrivelling under the hostile glare.

'Anyone who works for me should always be ready for trouble. Thousands of people are killed on the roads every day.'

Pawson seated himself opposite Reece and continued glowering. Reece tried to bear the scrutiny with outward aplomb, wondering how road accidents had anything to do with Peters.

'Why do you think I flew you back to England?' Pawson asked abruptly, softening his tone slightly.

'I don't know, sir.'

'I'll tell you then. Peters was a good man, one of the very best when he was fully operational, and there's every indication that he's been killed. I don't want you killed as well.' Pawson flashed a wintry smile. 'Your fancy woman in Belem would probably object.'

Reece kept quiet, blushing despite himself. He knew it was far safer to leave the talking to Pawson.

'I've a plan to wrap up this whole sorry business,' his chief continued, a hint of smugness in his voice. 'A bloody marvellous plan, although I say so myself. We're going to send in a decoy, someone entirely unconnected with the department who knows nothing about the cocaine and nothing about us. He'll be our personal puppet, primed to ask all the questions which should bring the opposition down on his head like a ton of bricks.' There was genuine pleasure in Pawson's smile on this occasion. 'When it happens you're going to be there, safely out of the firing line. Naturally, you'll do your best to prevent anything too unpleasant happening to our friend but that's secondary. Passing back the information comes first.'

As the germ of a plan the idea appealed to Reece, especially the part about him being out of the firing line. Unfortunately he could see several insurmountable snags which doomed it to failure. Not that he dared to say as much to Pawson, who was awaiting some comment.

'There are a couple of points I'd like to raise, sir,' he said deferentially, toning down the strength of his objections.

'Go ahead.'

Pawson was feeling expansive now.

'Firstly, we can't be certain Peter's disappearance has anything to do with the cocaine.'

'There are enough indications to make it extremely likely,' Pawson answered confidently. 'Some action has to be taken and we can't afford to be half-hearted about it. What's the other thing bothering you?'

'Where on earth are we going to find someone to act as decoy?' Reece asked, getting to the crux of the problem.

Pawson picked up a file from his desk, a faint smile on his lips.

'It's all in here,' he said, tapping the folder. 'You'll find it makes interesting reading. The subject's name is Philis and at the moment he's running a lucrative little racket in the Santos dock area. Perhaps you've already heard of him?'

Reece shook his head, still disenchanted with his chief's scheme. Set a thief to catch a thief might be a fine maxim in theory, but Reece didn't want to be around when an attempt was made to translate it into practice. Something of what he was feeling must have been mirrored in his expression.

'Don't underestimate Philis,' Pawson warned him sharply. 'Peters knew him well and was sufficiently impressed to suggest I recruited him. In fact he seemed to think Philis was tailor-made for SR(2). I chose to ignore the recommendation but that doesn't mean Philis is any ordinary crook. A lot of people objected to him setting up shop in Santos, but he's still there, and prospering.'

'What makes you think he'll want to work for us?' Reece asked, deciding he liked Philis less the more he heard about him.

Once again Pawson smiled.

'Don't worry,' he assured Reece. 'Philis will be only too glad to help Queen and country. Especially when he learns what I've got on him.'

CHAPTER I

IT WAS ONLY just after nine in the morning but the sun was already beating down, its harsh glare doing a power of no good for my head. I also had a guilty conscience to keep me company, realizing Laurena was going to be a trifle choked when she woke up to find I'd gone. It was the first time I'd been near her for a month, something which had taken a bit of explaining the night before, and she'd be justifiably upset by my desertion. After all, she was the one who'd set up my little deal with the steward of the *Oriole* the previous day. For ten cases of Black and White at four dollars a bottle she deserved a little more consideration, even if my profit was going to be in cruzeiros. Money apart, she was a sexy little piece, not much of a figure, or a face come to that, but in bed, where it counted, she knew what it was all about. I promised myself I'd pop down to see her some time in the next few days, just to show my appreciation.

The General Camera was slowly coming to life as I meandered along the uneven, pothole-scarred sidewalk. The corrugated metal shutters of the bars were being pushed up, sleepy-looking hostesses were drifting to work in ones and twos, and a few early birds among the beggars had taken up their pitches, offering their sore-covered limbs to the doubtful sympathy of the handful of sailors who were up and about.

I could have done with a shave and hot towel massage to freshen myself up but Garcia's shutter was still in place, so I carried my hangover a yard or two farther to the Stockholm Bar. Inside it was pleasantly dark and I cautiously eased my eyes open from the bloodshot slits they'd been in the street, feeling the big overhead fan get to work on my sweat-drenched brow. The day-shift girls were already on duty, drinking coffee round one of the tables and running down the mugs who'd shared their beds the night before, and I raised a limp hand in greeting before going to the bar. Paulista ran an experienced eye over me as I approached, making an instant diagnosis. By the time I'd perched on a stool he had a stiff cuba libre ready on the counter and was reaching for the phial of benzedrine. I thanked him, took a long swallow to wash down one of the tablets, then sat back, waiting for it to take effect.

It was nice and peaceful in the bar, no music and no women pestering me, and this was why I patronized the Stockholm, my one haven along the strip. With all the juggling around I had to do, I needed a retreat where I could relax over a quiet drink.

Half-way down the glass the benzedrine began to hit my system. My eyes came into focus, my hands stopped shaking and I started to forget I'd only had about five hours' sleep out of the last forty-eight. The past ten days had sucked me completely dry, with seven of my ships coming into Santos. What with entertaining contacts on board and buttering up the girls who'd put me in touch with them I'd put in more hours than I cared to remember. I was seriously considering the possibility of a well-earned holiday when both western style swing doors crashed back against the wall, the sudden noise lifting me six inches from my seat.

'I'm looking for a fight,' the drunk said in English, standing just out of range of the wildly vibrating doors.

He was big, topping six feet, and the sweaty T-shirt he was wearing did nothing to hide his muscles. I'd been in Rio in '66 when the Canadian Navy had gone through the red light district like a small hurricane and I recognized the expression on his face only too well. He'd hit Santos after a fortnight or so at sea, drunk cheap liquor until it was pouring out of his ears, picked up one of the freelance tarts and woken up in the morning to find his wallet gone. Now he was all set to take it out of the first person he met.

'I'm looking for a fight,' he repeated.

26

As a simple statement of intent he evidently didn't think this could be bettered. Looking round the bar, I had no difficulty in sorting out the chief contenders. The sailor didn't strike me as a woman-fighter so that just left Paulista or myself, and Paulista was already sliding through the door behind the bar. Simply because he'd been feeding me free drinks for the last few years Paulista seemed to think I ought to act as part-time bouncer.

'Don't look at me,' I told the sailor, who was now no more than five or six feet away. 'I'd hate you to damage your knuckles on my face.'

He kept on coming, prompting me to get off the bar stool.

'Anyway, I was just going,' I added, skirting him as I headed for the exit. 'It's been a privilege to make your acquaintance.'

My preparations for retreat earned catcalls of disapproval from the girls, their chairs already shifted so they could watch the fun, and the sailor didn't appreciate the move either. A large, grease-grimed hand shot out, the fingers hooking painfully into the flesh of my shoulder.

'I don't like you,' he anounced simply, drawing back his free hand.

Now he mentioned it I didn't like the idea of his ham-sized fist getting as far as my chin, not just when the benzedrine was working, so I grabbed the arm holding my shoulder, did a nifty half-turn and threw the sailor over the bar. He hit the slat board on the far side with an almighty thump, the air turning blue as he struggled back to his feet. The general idea seemed to be to tear off my arms and legs before he used his foot to re-site my tackle between my buttocks. This left me absolutely cold, not turning me on at all, and when his head came above the level of the bar I hit it with the stool I happened to have handy. Abruptly the swearing stopped, the girls turned back to their gossip and I lit a Louis XV.

Peace and tranquillity were restored to the Stockholm Bar, but not for long. Watched by an approving Paulista, I was industriously hauling the sailor from behind the bar when the police arrived, three of them, all with their riot sticks in evidence. I dropped the unconscious man before the first policeman could crack me on the wrist and leapt agilely to the bar before either of the others could prod me in the kidneys, leaning on it at the correct angle with my feet and hands well apart. One of them went over me for weapons, doing his damnedest to provoke me so they could all have a go with their lead-weighted batons. I didn't dare blink an eyelid, not even when he tried the standard trick of squeezing hard between my legs. Disappointed, the policeman jerked me back on to my feet.

'Let's go,' he said, pointing his riot stick towards the door.

His two companions were over with the women, their hands moving busily while they grabbed as much as possible before they left. It was an opportunity for me to scrutinize the policeman with me, wondering whether it was better to offer him a bribe or to wait until we reached the jail and I could get word to Inspector Pinto. As a result of my examination I decided to wait. Ninety per cent of the Brazilian police accepted bribes as a matter of course, the remainder were just looking for an excuse to commit legal murder. I unhesitatingly placed the one who'd searched me among the minority.

As soon as we drove away from the Stockholm and I had a chance to mull things over I realized there was something very wrong. In fact the whole affair stank to high heaven. For a start I knew all the men patrolling the dock area, had several of them on my payroll, yet the three sharing the van with me were all complete strangers. If this was unusual, the incident in the bar had been positively weird. A drunken sailor had walked in, had deliberately picked a fight with me, and lo and behold, a posse of policemen had been lurking outside, all ready to cart me off in a conveniently parked van. Come to think of it, they hadn't even bothered to move the sailor from where I'd dumped him on the floor.

Ten minutes later I was certain my custodians weren't

28

policemen at all, for wherever else we might be going, we were way, way off course for police headquarters. Policemen or not, they still had their riot sticks and guns so I decided I wouldn't tax them with the deception. Instead I sat back and did my best to enjoy the ride. Not being a masochist I didn't find this easy.

We were on the road for a little under half an hour, my calculations placing us in Sao Vicente by the time we stopped. A quick glimpse of the big suspension bridge as I was hustled out of the van confirmed this suspicion and the house I'd been brought to confirmed another. It was one of the small, white stucco villas which proliferated in the suburbs of any Brazilian city, bars over the windows to deter intruders and a six-foot hedge round the miniscule garden to maintain privacy. Inside there was the stale smell peculiar to houses that haven't been lived in for some time, dustcovers over the furniture to prove it. The men in fancy dress shoved me along a short corridor and into a room at the end of it where they left me. A crafty peek through the keyhole told me there was no guard posted outside the door but this omission didn't tempt me to try walking out again. I preferred to take a look through the window instead. Apart from a couple of palm trees, some highly coloured shrubs, which definitely weren't roses or buttercups, and a good view of the thick hedge a few feet away there was nothing to see.

The room itself showed more signs of recent habitation than the other parts of the building I'd seen, for while it wasn't exactly homely, the dustcovers had been pulled off two chairs and the table. The most interesting feature, however, was the newspaper lying on the table. I would have expected to find the *Estado de Sao Paulo* but this was a four-day-old edition of *The Times*, the genuine, home-grown article, not the flimsy edition. It was well over a year since I'd last seen an English newspaper, and for want of anything better to do, I settled down in the more comfortable of the two chairs to bring myself up

29

to date on how the mother country was getting along without me. Badly was my immediate impression, the main news amply justifying my self-imposed exile. Religious warfare in Northern Ireland, hooliganism on the football terraces, old age pensioners freezing to death and the rest of the country on strike, it all made me proud to be British. At least in Brazil they had won the World Cup, even if they were torturing political prisoners, kidnapping foreign ambassadors and petrol-bombing American-owned businesses.

I was just becoming absorbed in the football reports when the door opened. A man in civilian clothes stood on the threshold for a moment, examining me while I sat in my chair and stared right back. I'd seen myself in the mirror enough times to know he was getting the better of the deal. He was one of the smooth, nondescript, chinless wonders who characterized the British upper classes, whereas I was endowed with the kind of rugged good looks many a film star would envy. Considering the temperature was hovering around the hundred mark, with the humidity not far behind, the natty dark suit he was wearing displayed a superb disdain for climatic conditions. On the other hand, the gun he had in a shoulder-holster did make a jacket something of a necessity.

'You look bloody awful, Philis,' he said by way of an introduction.

Stuck for an appropriate answer I maintained a dignified silence. The remark had been designed to throw me off-balance and I didn't want anyone to know how successful it had been.

'It's high time you started taking things easier,' he went on. 'If those bags under your eyes grow any more they'll end up as double cheeks.'

He was quite the little joker, a laugh every minute, and I could feel my heart warming to him.

'Very droll,' I said. 'Just who the hell are you? And why the charade to bring me here?'

He smiled at me, revealing a set of even white teeth

which I'd have liked to believe had been provided courtesy of the National Health.

'The name is Reece,' he answered easily, 'and the charade, as you called it, was intended to cover up for your sudden departure from Santos.'

He awaited my reaction with interest, well aware that he had me at sixes and sevens. There were so many questions needing to be asked I didn't know where to begin.

'I've a job for you,' Reece continued when I made no comment. 'It's honest employment so it should make a pleasant change.'

'I won't tell you what you can do with your job,' I sneered, pushing myself out of the chair. 'I realize you're probably an expert already.'

I made resolutely for the door, although I had no intention of leaving—Reece had me far too interested for that. The idea was to discover whether he was really prepared to haul out his gun. When he did I stopped immediately.

'Who are you trying to fool?' I asked, sneering again. 'You're not going to shoot anyone. I don't work too well with bullet holes in me. The blood tends to leak out.'

'There's nothing to stop me bouncing the gun off your head, though,' Reece pointed out. 'And that's exactly what I intend to do if you try to walk through the door before I've had my say.'

Perhaps there was more to him than met the eye. I thought I could take Reece, but he evidently thought the same about me, which made us even. He wasn't putting on an act either. There was no bravado about him, only an air of calm competence to indicate he'd been in similar situations before. Mature consideration decided me it would be a painful business learning which of us was right so I returned to my seat and lit a cigarette.

'I deplore violence,' I told him, 'so have your say. It won't alter the fact I don't need a job, for you or anyone else.'

These noble sentiments didn't take the whiphand from

Reece. He dumped himself in the other chair and lit a cigarette of his own, a Senior Service. Evidently he had come into Brazil with the newspaper.

'Don't think I relish the prospect of employing a parasite like you,' he started, off on the flattery jag again, 'and I appreciate the fact that the thought of an honest day's work must come as a hell of a shock. After all, you have managed nine years in Brazil without any visible source of income.'

'I'm a man of means,' I lied. 'A rich aunt left me a legacy.'

'Come off it,' Reece said disgustedly. 'I know all about you. Quite honestly I can't imagine you being anyone's favourite nephew.'

The last remark was definitely below the belt, even if it was true. The only aunt I'd met had expended so much energy hiking backwards and forwards to the corner off-licence that she hadn't had enough left over to lavish affection on me. When she eventually died, the only legacy I could bank on was a cellar full of empties.

'You came to Brazil in 1962, purportedly to work for the Five Star Shipping Company in Porto Alegre.' After a deep drag at his cigarette Reece had started on my life story. 'You lasted a whole week before you resigned, and if you hadn't taken the initiative, the odds were against you, lasting a fortnight in any case. While you were finding your feet you lived at the expense of one Rita Valdez, a wealthy Argentinian divorcee with a predilection for virile young Europeans.'

He threw me a quizzical glance, as if to ask how I fell into this category. Stony-faced, I let the insult to my manhood slide, once again finding myself without a suitable riposte.

'Using money borrowed from her,' Reece went on, 'you began to play the dollar black market, ditching the woman as soon as you'd accumulated enough capital. You never did pay back the money you'd borrowed.'

'I didn't borrow it,' I said, stung into self-defence. 'She gave me the money.'

Reece had the bones of the story substantially correct but he'd painted the picture far blacker than it had actually been. In reality Rita and I had parted the best of friends. She'd found herself a seven-foot Swedish basketball player and I'd had one or two women lined up as a contingency reserve.

'Either way makes you a gigolo,' Reece pointed out pleasantly. 'Anyway, you kept on dabbling in currency until Goulart was given the boot and the military junta brought in more stringent financial regulations. Even so, you managed to make a packet out of the 1966 revaluation. In general, however, you went through a thin spell, living off capital apart from the occasional odd job, usually of a dubious nature.'

Reece paused to see if I was still listening.

'Do you agree with me so far?' he inquired.

'Let's put it this way,' I answered, impressed by his research. 'I'm not going to argue with you.'

'I didn't think you would,' Reece purred, a smug expression on his face. 'Eventually, of course, you ran out of funds. Then you took to smuggling in a small way, mostly liquor and cigarettes. Porto Alegre wasn't a big enough port for you to make a really fat living, but the profit margins were good and it was an ideal training for when you moved to Santos.'

He stopped again, treating me to an apologetic glance.

'That's the one blank in the narrative, I'm afraid. You left Porto Alegre in a hell of a rush and I haven't been able to dig up the reason. Perhaps you'd like to tell me.'

'I don't like,' I said bluntly.

He'd struck on an extremely raw nerve. I'd been run out of Porto Alegre on the traditional rail, given twenty-four hours to leave town by a man I wouldn't choose to argue with unless I had a brigade or two of commandos to back me up.

'No matter,' Reece droned on, unabashed by my uncommunicativeness. 'You came to Santos and really refined your operation. All the tarts on the General Camera had regular customers on the ships docking here, so you spent a couple of months buttering them up. They introduced you to seamen and officers who didn't mind having a little extra money in their pockets and you took it from there. At first it was alcohol and cigarettes again, then you diversified as you developed your outlets and established yourself with the local police. You're still not big time but you'd be way up in the surtax bracket in England.'

For the time being Reece had finished, which was just as well because I'd had more than enough. He might have done his homework well but this wasn't getting us anywhere.

'In case you didn't know I'm quite an expert on my own life story,' I told him. 'If you think you can blackmail me into working for you, you've gone to a lot of trouble for nothing. I'm absolutely solid with the police.'

The information upset Reece so much he couldn't stop himself from smiling.

'Blackmail doesn't come into it,' he said. 'When I called you a parasite I didn't say you weren't an intelligent parasite. I'm perfectly well aware that you never take a step without buying immunity beforehand. The only reason I've catalogued your career in Brazil so fully is to show how thoroughly you've been investigated. Before I say what I want you to do I'd better tell you I'm willing to pay five hundred pounds for your services. Two hundred and fifty pounds now, the rest when the assignment is over.'

The offer prompted me to laugh in his face.

'You can stop there,' I told him. 'Whatever the job, that isn't anywhere enough to make me want to work for you.'

'In that case,' Reece said softly, 'would it make any difference if I told you Otto Schmidt was in trouble?'

The room went quiet, the snarl of traffic on the road outside the only sound to intrude on my thoughts, for Otto Schmidt was the best friend I was ever likely to have, despite the difference in our respective ages. We'd met shortly after my arrival in Porto Alegre, bumping into

34

each other in the Je Reviens Bar. He was a German who had come to Porto Alegre after the war and established a thriving restaurant, the top eating place in a city renowned for its food. This had meant there was more than the generation gap for our friendship to surmount, as my social status was way down the scale. Surprisingly enough, neither factor had mattered, simply because we'd enjoyed each other's company, and, by the time I'd left for Santos, we'd become all but inseparable.

Friendship apart, I was deeply in Otto's debt. Some of my dealings had brought me into contact with local political figures, not all of them wisely chosen. When Goulart had been overthrown, Porto Alegre, one of his main centres of support, had become a very dodgy place to be in if you'd associated with the wrong people. I had, and my name figured prominently on the shortlist of undesirable aliens. Otto had refused to tell me how much it had cost him when he'd arranged to have it removed, but I knew it must have been a substantial amount. I certainly owed him a favour in return, just so long as I didn't have to return to Porto Alegre.

'Go on,' I said to Reece. 'I'm interested now.'

Although he hadn't shown it Reece must have been tense because now he visibly relaxed.

'How much do you know about Schmidt?' he asked.

'I haven't seen him since I left PA but I think I know him as well as anyone.'

'I'll rephrase the question. What do you know about Schmidt's life in Germany before he came to Brazil?'

'Nothing,' I answered immediately. 'Otto never talked about Germany and I didn't ask any questions. He gave me the impression that he'd had a rough time during the war.'

'You could say that.' Reece flashed a wry grin. 'Among other things, he was an officer in the SS and, under his real name of Franz Gottfried, he was listed by the War Crimes Commission. Part of his trouble is that the Israelis are on his trail.'

Part of Reece's trouble was that he was an incurable optimist. As a mental exercise I tried to reconcile the Otto Schmidt I knew and liked with Franz Gottfried, war criminal, but the two images just didn't tally. Otto undoubtedly had secrets in his past, everyone had them, and I'd have wagered my life savings that being a Nazi war criminal wasn't one of them. Apparently Reece thought I was so dazzled with the amount he'd dug up about me that I'd accept any crap he was prepared to offer. Later he was due for a grave disappointment, for the time being I wanted to hear what else he had to say.

'You said the Israelis were part of his problem,' I prompted. 'What's the rest of it?'

'All in good time. To start with, I'd better explain that I represent the British Treasury.'

I'd noticed before how fond Reece was of significant pauses. He popped one in now to see how impressed I was by the information and my offkey whistled rendition of 'Land of Hope and Glory' seemed like an adequate answer.

'You don't believe me?' Reece was surprised.

'Of course I do,' I assured him. 'All the Civil Servants I know wear guns. Or perhaps you were planning to rob the Banco do Brasil while you're here, just to ease the balance of payments situation?'

Reece reached into his inside jacket pocket, bringing out a small, red plastic wallet which he handed to me. Inside there was a natty little card, complete with photograph, informing me that Paul Reece worked for the Investigation Branch of HM Treasury.

'Very nice,' I said admiringly. 'I can't think of more than a dozen places in Santos where this might have been made. I'd rather see your passport, and your Carteira de Identidade if you have one.'

With a shrug of his shoulders Reece delved into his pocket again, producing the documents I'd requested. Both of them bore out what he'd told me, otherwise he wouldn't have allowed me to see them, and from his passport I learned he'd arrived in Rio three days previously.

36

'OK,' I conceded. 'Let's pretend you really are a Treasury official. What's the connection with Otto and the Israelis you say he has on his tail?'

'It's quite straightforward,' Reece explained, making me grin in anticipation. 'For nearly a year we've known there's been a high-class counterfeiting ring operating somewhere in South America. The bulk of the forgeries have been American 10- and 20-dollar bills, with only a few forged five-pound notes coming on the market, probably because sterling isn't a very popular currency over here. Naturally US Treasury and FBI men have been swarming all over the place, and we ourselves have been investigating on a more modest scale, but until recently we didn't even know which country the forgeries were coming from. They were being passed across the counter in every large South American city and there wasn't a single substantial lead to help us. As you can imagine, it was a worrying situation, especially as the forgeries were of such a high quality. Whoever is behind the operation wasn't being particularly greedy but month by month the total mounted. We eventually managed to stop the flow through the banks, then, three months ago, forged currency started to turn up on the eastern seaboard of the United States and the counterfeit bills indubitably came from the same source. None of the phoney fivers have been spotted for some time but we're not kidding ourselves. Unless we locate the plates it won't be very long before they do.'

When Reece had finished I didn't bother to stifle a yawn. I'd stopped believing in fairy tales at the age of five, just as soon as I'd realized the wicked witches and ogres didn't stand a chance.

'Absolutely fascinating,' I commented. 'Wake me up when you reach the relevant part.'

'I'm coming to the point. Four weeks ago an envelope was hand delivered to the Embassy in Rio. Inside was one of the counterfeit fivers and a note saying that if we were interested we should place an advertisement in the next day's edition of the *Estado de Sao Paulo*. The exact

37

wording to be used was provided. We inserted the ad as specified and the would-be informant contacted the Embassy again, by phone this time. It took a week for both sides to establish bona fides and guarantees, then our informant identified himself—Otto Schmidt. He wanted a British passport, secure passage to the destination of his choice and five thousand pounds in cash. In return he would supply sufficient information to smash the counterfeiting ring.'

'And Otto casually mentioned the Israelis were after him?' I asked, still wondering how gullible Reece thought I was.

'He did,' Reece agreed, insulting my intelligence a bit more. 'I told you that we spent a week establishing bona fides. Everything he told us checked out.'

'All right. Just where do I come into the picture?'

'Schmidt specified you as go-between, otherwise there was no deal. As a close friend of his you could visit him without arousing any suspicion and he said you owed him a favour. In fact we were about to contact you two weeks ago when we had a setback.'

'What was that?' I asked.

Unless I prompted Reece with the obvious questions I was afraid I might hurt his feelings.

'Schmidt disappeared, completely vanished. He may have gone into hiding, the Israelis could have grabbed him, though that seems unlikely, or his forging friends may have become suspicious. We just don't know.'

There was yet another pause, presumably to build up what Reece imagined to be suspense.

'You're the man we want to go to Porto Alegre and find out what's happened. You know your way around down there, people will remember you as Schmidt's friend and you're the man he wants to see. If he's dead or languishing in Tel Aviv jail you'll be earning your money for nothing and we'll have to saturate the area to run down Schmidt's contacts. Before we do this we want to make absolutely sure that the original deal can't be swung.'

Reece stopped and watched me expectantly, waiting for me to jump at his offer. Either he was deranged, naïve or had a misplaced faith in his own persuasiveness. Personally I thought he'd pushed so much bull it was a wonder his eyeballs hadn't turned brown, and I'd read books by Enid Blyton which had been a hell of a sight more convincing. The only solid fact to emerge was that Otto had to be in trouble, and, regrettably, there was nothing I could do to help him. He was my friend and I owed him a lot, there was no denying this, but I didn't owe him my life. This was exactly what I stood to forfeit if I ever returned to Porto Alegre.

'It's not on,' I told Reece. 'You yourself admitted I might have a little intelligence and intelligent people don't become involved with gangs of international forgers, not to mention Israeli agents. You could offer me ten thousand pounds, with an autographed photograph of Ted Heath thrown in, and I still wouldn't be interested. Either Otto fends for himself or you'll have to persuade someone else to look for him. And that's final.'

For a moment Reece sat motionless, then he smiled, a slow smile which made my toenails curl. He slipped his hand inside his jacket but instead of a gun his hand reappeared holding nothing more dangerous than a manilla envelope. Casually he skimmed it along the table, aiming at my left elbow.

'Earlier I told you I didn't intend to use blackmail to force you to work for me,' he said pleasantly. 'I've just changed my mind.'

Reluctantly I looked inside the envelope. It contained the photostat of a cheque, drawn on the Banco Nacional de Minas Gerais and payable to me, all innocent enough except for one small detail. The cheque had been signed by A. F. Barras.

CHAPTER II

FORTY-FIVE MINUTES later I picked up a taxi outside the villa and directed the driver back into Santos. There was £250 sterling in a trouser pocket and Reece's explicit instructions contained in my head, along with the bitter knowledge that I was finished in Brazil. Much as I disliked Reece I had to admit he was a marvellous blackmailer and, quite frankly, I couldn't understand how on earth he'd come up with the photostat. Caution being my watchword, I'd taken only one real risk in all my years in Brazil and, curiously enough, Otto had been involved in this incident as well. A couple of months or so after he'd smoothed over the deportation threat, a time when my funds had been at a drastically low ebb, Otto had told me he knew of something he could put my way if I was interested, a man who'd been connected with the Goulart administration and who wanted to be slipped over the Uruguayan border. Normally I wouldn't have touched the job with a disinfected barge pole and I was even less inclined to take it when I realized who was involved. Barras had been one of Goulart's top men, a power behind the throne, and the military junta responsible for the revolution were all set to lock him away for the odd century or two once they laid hands on him. Eventually the amount of money I was promised proved too great a temptation and, with grave forebodings, I agreed to deliver him to Montevideo. Unexpectedly, the trip turned out to be a doddle, with no hitches until I tried to collect my rake-off, the payment for services rendered consisting of 150 dollars in American currency and a cheque for the balance drawn on a Brazilian bank. It was a beautiful swindle. Barras had lived up to the letter of the agreement, only we both knew the cheque was absolutely worthless. The first thing the new régime had done was

40

to start checking the bank accounts of all Goulart's known associates and I couldn't afford to become involved. For some time I'd kept the cheque, on the off-chance Barras would return to favour, but when the newspapers began citing him as the author of various guerrilla raids in Rio Grande do Sul I'd promptly destroyed it. The photostat in Reece's possession showed I'd delayed the precaution for too long. Despite the years that had elapsed, I knew the Brazilian authorities would still feel plenty of illwill towards the man who'd helped Barras out of the country.

Faced with such a potent threat I'd had no alternative to accepting Reece's proposition, hence the £250 and the instructions. Basically I didn't have many objections, especially as doing as Reece wanted would mean the photostat wouldn't be used and I'd be able to stay in Santos. Brazil was my adopted country, the country I'd chosen to live in and the one I wanted to continue living in. Moreover Otto was my best friend and I'd have liked to bail him out of the trouble he was in. The snag was the man in Porto Alegre who, at our last encounter, had done more than hint at how unhealthy it would be for me to set foot in the city again. This had been no idle threat and the prospect of being killed didn't appeal to me any more than a prolonged spell in a Brazilian jail. My mind was made up. Caracas was a town I'd always had a yen to visit, especially as I'd never heard of anyone being extradited from Venezuela.

However, there was too much at stake for me to go off at half cock. Now I knew how dangerous Reece could be a few precautions didn't seem out of order and I had the driver take me down the Ana Costa, through the tunnel and into the centre of Santos, making him drive slowly. The tactic didn't gain me much. There was a steady stream of traffic into the city, three-quarters of the cars on the road being Brazilian-made Volkswagens, and it was impossible to tell whether I was being tailed or not. In the Praca Maua, which was within easy walking distance of my apartment on the Frei Gasper, I paid off

41

the taxi, using the excuse of buying a newspaper to have another look around. The result was still inconclusive and I strolled across the square in the direction of Lojas Americanas, the Brazilian Woolworths. The store was ideal for my purposes, the ground floor jampacked with shoppers, and, once inside, I abandoned all pretence of being casual, trampling old women and children underfoot as I made for the exit on the far side of the shop. Through the doors I ignored the passing stream of taxis, ducked into the entrance of the office building twenty yards down the street and ran up the first flight of stairs. There was a comfortable-looking, green leather couch in the corridor and the building was air-conditioned so I sat down to smoke a couple of cigarettes.

By the time I'd finished the second my shirt had dried out nicely. The effects of my early morning benzedrine were beginning to wear off as well, not tempting me to rush around in the blazing, noon-day sun. Accordingly, I took the stairs at a more leisurely pace before walking down into Lojas Americanas. On this return visit I oozed sociably through the crowd, patting small children on the head and smiling at the attractive negress assistants, until I reached the last counter before the Praca Maua entrance. Although my precautions were probably superfluous by now I was taking no chances and I radiated relaxed insouciance as I examined the selection of plastic handbags, none of which would have gone with my hand-stitched shoes.

There was a gaggle of customers coming through the door when the first open-sided tram went by but I had a clear run at the second. It had to slow down to take the corner leaving the square and I started off like a greyhound, covering the ten yards or so at top speed before I leaped lithely on to the step running the whole length of the tram. Round the next corner, some two hundred yards away, I dropped off again, ignoring the angry shouts of the conductor who'd been struggling towards me, intent on collecting my fare. Less than thirty seconds later I was in a taxi heading back to the beach. Anyone who was still with me deserved a medal and Reece couldn't possibly know about my second apartment on the Rua Maranhao.

Miguel, the zelador of the apartment building, sat comfortably at the top of the steps and watched me cross the pavement towards him, eyes bulging over the litre bottle of cerveja he was draining. With a last gurgle he killed the bottle and was wiping his thick lips with the back of his hand when I reached him.

'Hallo, gringo,' he said, putting heavy emphasis on the second word to make sure I wouldn't miss the insult.

'Cut it, you black ape,' I answered. 'If you can't keep a civil tongue in your head I'll have to have a word with the landlord.'

'I'm sorry, Senhor Philis,' he said penitently, all contrition.

We both laughed. Miguel owned the whole shebang, right up to the fifteenth floor, and had enough money in the bank to keep me in luxury for the rest of my life. The reason he didn't indulge himself more was that he was too bloody idle. He preferred to spend twelve hours a day basking in the sun as nominal concierge, doing a job he could have hired someone else to do for a handful of cruzeiros. The other twelve hours he spent shacked up in his penthouse with his wife, the kind ol lush Copacabana mulatto that has the tourists flocking to Rio.

'Have you kept the flat nicely aired?' I asked.

It was more than a month since I'd last used it.

'I have,' he answered. 'A woman cleans up a couple of times a week and I make sure she doesn't walk off with anything. Your visitor should find everything spick and span.'

'My visitor?' I said blankly, doing a double-take.

'Your English friend,' Miguel explained patiently. 'He's been waiting in the flat for more than half an hour.'

Reluctantly I chalked up another point to Reece. He'd not only unearthed my bolt hole but he'd correctly anticipated my reactions. The man was beginning to frighten me a little. Although I knew I was brighter than the average bear Reece had me outgunned all along the line. So far anyway.

'Miguel,' I said with commendable calm, 'my English visitor isn't a friend at all. I wasn't expecting any callers.'

Miguel's face fell tragically. I could see he felt he'd let me down.

'I'm sorry, Philis,' he said miserably. 'He let himself straight into your apartment. I thought you must have given him the spare key.'

'Not to worry,' I said quickly, patting him on the shoulder. 'There's no real harm done.'

As I explained what I had in mind Miguel brightened up considerably. In fact he was so enthusiastic he didn't resent leaving his comfortable seat and hiking all of five yards to the lift.

My plan was simplicity itself. Appropriating Miguel's empty beer bottle I took the service lift at the back of the building to the ninth floor, soft footed it up to the floor above, where my apartment was, and parked myself outside the tradesman's entrance. A couple of minutes later I heard the main lift ascending with Miguel inside, armed with my front door key. I waited until he started fumbling with the lock, then I noiselessly unlocked the kitchen door. Reece was standing with his back to me, peering round the edge of the door connecting the kitchen with the living-room and evidently expecting me to walk through the front door at any second. I really hated to disappoint him but I broke the bottle over his head just the same.

The first indication of Reece's return to consciousness was a groan. It wasn't much of a groan so I stayed out on the balcony overlooking the beach, sipping at the outsize batida which was rapidly taking over where the benzedrine had left off. In the next five minutes the groans became more heartfelt and increased in authority. Judging the time was ripe I lit a Bahian cigar, collected the jug of melted ice from the kitchen and poured the contents over Reece's head. After a lot of spluttering and some language which should have had him out of the Civil Service like a shot Reece succeeded in pushing himself into a sitting position, one hand tenderly clutching the back of his head.

'I didn't think you'd still be here,' he said thickly, droplets of iced water trickling from his nose and chin.

'Nor did I,' I told him, helping him up and steering him to the sofa. 'Apparently I do have a conscience after all. Luckily it's not so highly developed that it'll stop me from belting you again and heading for pastures green unless you come up with a hell of a sight better story than the one you fed me at the villa.'

Reece sat on the edge of the sofa, his head held in his hands while he thought things over. I didn't rush him. As far as I could remember I'd never felt too good immediately after being hit on the head with a bottle. Eventually he raised his head but he still wasn't ready. We passed some more time, me puffing at my cigar and Reece staring fixedly at the coffee table.

'I thought *Playboy* was banned over here,' he said at last, pointing to where the magazine lay on the table.

'It probably is.'

There was no need to explain. It was pleasant to think there was at least one of my deals, however small, that Reece didn't know about.

'I'm still waiting,' I said after another two or three minutes had gone by.

'All right, Philis. I suppose you deserve the full story though my boss will have my guts for garters if he ever finds out. The thing I omitted to tell you earlier was that Schmidt is working for us. Or rather he's been seconded to the Treasury from MI6. He's been acting as observer for them ever since nineteen forty-eight. Incidentally, you'd be surprised how many war criminals there are working for British intelligence. They make ideal agents.'

Of course I'd be surprised, the same way I'd be surprised if a word Reece had told me turned out to be true. It was a new story all right but this didn't mean I had to believe it.

'Since when has Porto Alegre been a nerve centre of the cold war?' I asked. 'I know damn all about the workings of British intelligence but I do know that a permanent agent based there would be the biggest waste of money since the *Titanic*.'

'He'd be no use at all,' Reece agreed. 'As I said, Schmidt was only an observer. An honorary observer in view of his past.' A thin smile accompanied this remark. 'In the twenty-odd years he's been on MI6's books he hasn't done a thing beyond keeping London informed about people who might conceivably prove to be useful. On the other hand he was always there in case of emergency. This is the first time he's been operational.'

An unpleasant thought had taken root in my mind. I tried to dismiss it but it only grew stronger.

'Otto was the one who gave you all the information about me,' I suggested.

'That's right,' Reece confirmed. 'He spotted you as someone potentially useful. In his report he mentioned you weren't exactly a patriot and that the photostat might be helpful in winning you over. Always assuming you were ever needed, and at the time the prospect seemed pretty remote.'

I mulled things over. Reece's story, even in the present, revised version, still struck me as belonging to the world of fantasy. The one thing I really couldn't stomach was the global counterfeiting network. Subtly I intimated my doubts.

'I think the intenational forging part is a load of crap,' I said.

'It was a trifle exaggerated,' Reece admitted without a blush. 'It had to be if you were going to believe my original story. There really is some forging taking place in the

Porto Alegre area, though. That's why we borrowed Schmidt for a while. It didn't seem worthwhile sending someone all the way from England when we had a man on the spot, so to speak. It's only a pipsqueak operation, poor, forgeries and not many of them. So far, however, the local police have got nowhere and Schmidt has disappeared. We want you to find out what has happened to him while I link up with the police. It's as simple as that.'

Personally I didn't think it was at all simple and I wasn't any happier with Reece's new line than I'd been with the old. There was a false ring to it which would have made me discount the story completely if I hadn't known Reece was telling the truth about Otto's disappearance. I couldn't pinpoint what had stopped me packing and prompted me to make a couple of phone calls while Reece was unconscious but, whatever the reason, I was now stuck with the results. Otto had to be in bad trouble to cut himself off from the two men I'd rung, the knowledge leaving me with a straight choice. The easy way, the way I'd taken on every other occasion the question had arisen, was to head for Caracas and a fresh start. The hard way was to go back to Porto Alegre, not for Reece but to try to help Otto. And to salvage some self-respect. I'd been run out of Porto Alegre and I was blowed if I'd be run out of Brazil as well. It was my country and I liked it enough to make it worthwhile for me to fight to stay.

'You win,' I said grudgingly. 'I'll do my best to find Otto but if I'm successful don't expect me to come running straight to you. I'll want to hear what Otto has to say first.'

'Don't worry, Philis,' Reece told me with a tight grin. 'I'm going to Porto Alegre as well. I'll be around.'

CHAPTER III

SEEN FROM THE air Porto Alegre looked pretty much the same as when I'd last been there. Jutting out into the lagoon was the city's commercial centre, its eyecatching, multi-storied skyline enhanced by one or two recent additions. On the landward side the sprawling residential districts, gradually petering out into rural slums, probably covered a larger area but not enough to be readily noticeable. And across the river the suspension bridge was still standing, its graceful lines making Sydney harbour bridge look like a clumsy piece of Meccano. I had plenty of time to examine the city because the pilot muffed his first two approaches, offering unintelligible, metallic explanations over the tannoy. Not that this bothered me. I had absolute confidence in the efficiency of an airline that could dig up hostesses as attractive as the ones we had aboard.

To divert myself I filled in the extra time by endeavouring to spot the big, fancy cemetery which was another feature of the city. From the outside it had the appearance of a five star, rancho hotel, with its exotic gardens, sparkling fountains, long, cool verandahs and softly piped music. At night the cemetery was even floodlit. I knew exactly where it should be, up on the hill beside the Scirocco Club, but it was impossible to pick it out from the plane. Not that this really mattered, I was merely indulging a morbid fancy. Gordinho owned the Scirocco Club and if he intended to keep his word I ought to start thinking about booking a plot next door.

At ground level the city hadn't altered much either. The approaches to the city were still guarded by the statue commemorating the splendour of the gaucho, one of the sick jokes of all time. The average gaucho had the intelli-

gence you'd associate with someone who spent his entire
life chasing cows, smelled even worse than the tic-bitten
horse he rode and would cut his own mother's throat for
the price of a drink. Possibly the statue was intended as
a boundary line beyond which the gauchos were not to
pass for Porto Alegre was predominantly a German city.
This made it one of the cleanest, most modern cities in
Brazil, with the best beer in South America and the best
restaurants, shops and hotels in Brazil outside Rio and
Sao Paulo. At the same time it retained its peculiarly
Brazilian character, helped by the swarms of shoeshine
boys and beggars and by its ten thousand registered pros-
titutes out of a population of little over three quarters of
a million. It was a fair example of what the journalists
liked to call the two faces of Brazil. At the tip of the iceberg the lucky few enjoyed a standard of living comparable
to that in the capital cities of Europe while a much larger
portion of the population lived in the favellas on black
beans and rice, sending their daughters out on the street
when they were twelve. Not that I was complaining. I'd
long since forgotten what black beans tasted like and some
of the daughters were bloody attractive.

I booked into the Hotel Broadway, wishing I'd had
time to have some false documents manufactured. Lacking
them I had to use my real name and hope news of my
arrival took a long, long time to percolate through to
Gordinho. One point in my favour was that none of the
staff at reception knew me. It was a new hotel, not quite
up to the standard set by the City, Plaza or Everest but
still worthy of the odd star or two under the English ratings.

All in all it had been an exhausting day. After a shower
and an enormous churrascoed steak in the hotel restaurant
I went back to my room, more than ready for bed. The
brightly wrapped parcel on the bedside table woke me up
fast. Lighting a cigarette I sat down on the edge of the
bed, in no particular rush to open it. No one, not even
Reece, should know where I was staying and the unexpected present meant Gordinho's information service had

excelled itself. So much for my hopes of a day or two's grace.

Picking up the phone I had the operator put me through to reception. There I was told that the parcel had been brought in by the shoeshine boy whose pitch was outside the hotel. Without too many expectations I sent the receptionist to question him. All the boy could say was that a man had driven up in a Volkswagen and asked him to take the package into the hotel, telling him it was for Sr Philis in room 609. This didn't help me a bit but I thanked the receptionist for his trouble just the same. The way things were going I could do with a few friendly people around.

The parcel stayed on the table and I remained sitting on the bed, still feeling no great compulsion to open it. Not that it ticked or anything dramatic like this. It just rustled. There was obviously a box underneath the garish paper and inside the box was something which was alive. Knowing Gordinho for the simple fun lover he was it wasn't difficult to guess what it might be. My cigarette finished I went through to the bathroom, half filling the bath before I dropped in the parcel. Then I held it under the water for a good five minutes, watching the bubbles bursting to the surface, and allowed two more for good measure after they'd stopped. The plate-sized spider, with its obscene covering of black, bristly hairs, I flushed down the lavatory, the soggy card I took back into the bedroom to decipher. This didn't take me very long. 'Dear Philis,' it ran, 'I heard you were back in Porto Alegre. Take good care of yourself.' At the bottom were the X and thumbprint which constituted Gordinho's signature.

It was ludicrous, of course, but then everything about Gordinho was ludicrous except his ability to make money. Even the name everyone knew him by was a joke, a reference to the excessive amount of flesh he carted around on his large frame. Apart from his massive paunch he was famous for his total illiteracy, indubitable illegitimacy and the fact he was probably the most powerful man in southern Brazil. According to local legend he'd started in business some forty years before, selling rotten fruit from one rickety barrow. Now he was the largest fruit wholesaler in Porto Alegre, ran seven supermarkets, had a fifty-one per cent interest in a flourishing domestic airline and owned half a dozen night clubs.

For a man who couldn't write his own name this wasn't bad going and it was just my bad luck that I'd happened to lay his mistress. I'd know Gordinho by sight, having seen him several times at one of his night clubs or in the Je Reviens Bar, and had heard all about the female sex bomb he had set up in a bungalow near the Leopoldville Tennis Club. Unfortunately I hadn't connected the woman I'd met at the Mil et Um Noites with this information, although sex bomb was certainly an apt description of Giselle. Nor did either of us know Gordinho was so jealous of his proprietary rights that he had one of his men following her. The first inkling I'd had of impending trouble was when I was forcibly dragged to Gordinho's headquarters at the Scirocco Club, worked over by a couple of his goons and told by the man himself that it might not be a bad idea for me to be somewhere else by the next morning. It hadn't occurred to me to argue.

To judge by the contents of the parcel all was still not forgiven, no stretch of my imagination being able to describe it as a goodwill offering. On the credit side it had been more of an appetizer than a genuine attempt to dispose of me, although I might have been a hospital case if I'd been fool enough to open the package without precautions. Before I retired for the night I slipped my antique Colt under the pillow. Up to now I hadn't fired the thing and I hadn't used a hand gun since my first few months in Santos but there seemed to be a fair chance I'd soon get in some practice.

The last thing Gordinho could have expected was that I'd pay him a visit. This was why, bright and early the next morning, I took a taxi ride up to the Scirocco Club.

Seen from the road it appeared deceptively small, only the unlit neon sign on the white façade to show the club wasn't a private residence. Because the bottom half of the front was windowless and the only entrance was at the top of a steep flight of steps it gave the impression of being a single-storied building. It was also impossible to guess how far the premises stretched back from the road. In actual fact there were two floors and the place was a veritable rabbit warren. Apart from the two large rooms providing for drinking, dancing and propositioning the hostesses the club was large enough to include forty bedrooms for the girls and a personal suite for Gordinho. The club itself only operated between 9 p.m. and 4 a.m., after that all business was conducted in the rooms at the back, accompanied by a squeaking of laboured bedsprings. Considering the volume of trade it was surprising the whole building didn't quiver on its foundations.

With my taxi paid off I hiked up the wooden steps and pushed open the door to the club. Although the bar was deserted no one had bothered to lock the place, an indication of Gordinho's position in Porto Alegre. Only someone with a death wish would steal anything from him, the same way no one would dream of having it away with his mistress. Having done the one it didn't make much odds about doing the other and I hunted around the bar for a bottle of whisky, not the local rubbish but the genuine scotch Gordinho kept for his friends. Although I wasn't exactly a bosom buddy of his I knew it had to be there. After all, in the old days, I'd helped to supply him.

Twenty minutes later and a couple of good glassfuls down the bottle a car drew up outside. Before I heard the footsteps coming up the steps I knew it had to be Gordinho. One of his men had followed me from the Broadway and if Gordinho had already been on the premises I would have had company earlier. The ruddy great Colt jammed in my waistband was becoming uncomfortable so I slipped it out and had it down by my side when the outer door opened, allowing a group of men to come in. It took a second or two for their eyes to adjust to the dim light, an opportunity for me to look them over. Gordinho, of course, I recognised at once and he didn't seem a day older than when I'd last seen him. Even the crumpled, white suit he was wearing could have been the same one. He definitely missed out on the young, vital and alert category of businessman for, despite the years of success, he still looked more like a barrow boy than anything else. Apart from the cluster of expensive, ostentatious rings on his fingers, that is.

The three men who followed him in I'd never seen before, a preliminary survey not making me think the loss had been mine. They were all of a kind, lean, hard-eyed waterfront toughs who would think nothing of murder if it earned them enough for a square meal and a bottle of cachaca. Men who had come in from the outback to seek a livelihood in the big city, only to find the grinding poverty they'd come to escape. Someone who lived in the favellas couldn't be expected to hold life as anything but cheap. When the life under consideration was mine I begged to differ.

No one seemed particularly bothered with the niceties of social etiquette. I sat at the bar, clutching the gun in a damp hand, and watched the group just inside the door. They stood there and looked at me. The expression on Gordinho's seamed, peasant's face didn't suggest the return of the prodigal.

'Throw him out,' he said flatly, speaking to the hired assassins behind him.

There had obviously been a briefing prior to their arrival because between them they produced one length of lead piping, a baling hook and a machete. None of these were specifically designed to do me any good but the very thought of being worked over with a machete gave me the cold shivers. I raised my right hand from my side to show them the gun.

'Surprise, surprise,' I said pleasantly. 'The hero remembered to bring his trusty six shooter. It's loaded as well, just in case anyone's interested.'

They were interested all right, so much so that they shelved the idea of bouncing me out of the club. Instead the three hard cases concentrated exclusively on avoiding any move which might make me pull the trigger. A .45 is a big gun and if you're looking up the barrel it seems like a cannon, hence the sudden respect. Except from Gordinho, that is. He remained where he'd been standing since he'd come in, sizing me up. Apparently I looked as though I might be able to hit someone if I wanted to.

'Out,' Gordinho ordered his minions, jerking his thumb towards the door.

They responded to the command with alacrity, patently relieved not to have had an arm or leg shot off. Once they'd gone Gordinho strolled to the bar with his habitual, purposeful tread, aiming for a bar stool three away from mine.

'I hope you don't mind me sitting down,' he said when he'd made himself comfortable.

'Not at all,' I answered, resting the Colt on my knee and keeping the business end aimed at his navel, 'but I would take it as a personal favour if you'd have a word with the men you sent round the back. Just thinking about them gives me a nervous tic in my trigger finger.'

For the first time Gordinho's face registered more than an active dislike for me, the fractional lift of his eyebrows indicating his surprise. Nonetheless he was prepared to be co-operative and turned to tell the two men lurking in the shadows of the adjoining room that everything was under control. He also told them not to move too far away, a gentle reminder to me that it would be wiser not to try anything clever.

'You've grown up fast,' he said emotionlessly, returning his attention to me. 'How did you know they were there?'

I shrugged modestly.

'Common sense,' I told him. 'You obviously picked the other three characters straight out of the gutter on the way over here. The man who tailed me from the Broadway didn't come in with you, nor did your chauffeur. They had to be round the back.'

It was a nice fable, crediting me with plenty of cool, logical deduction, far better than admitting I'd caught a brief glimpse of the two men reflected in the mirror behind the bar. Even so Gordinho wasn't impressed.

'Why did you come back here?' he asked. 'I thought I'd made my attitude plain at our last meeting.'

'You did,' I assured him, fingering the small scar above my left eye which was a momento of the occasion. 'The present you sent me last night showed you hadn't changed your mind. I must admit I was impressed with the speed your boys picked me up.'

'I like to know who's in town,' he said in a matter of fact voice, left cold by my delicate flattery. 'And I'm still waiting to learn why you've returned to Porto Alegre. Surely you're not stupid enough to think you can start up here again.'

'No, I'm settled in Santos now. I came here to ask you to leave me alone for three days, then I'll be gone.'

Gordinho sat impassively on his stool, no hint of his thoughts reflected in his face. He'd have made a great poker player.

'Why should I?' he enquired, keeping strictly to the point.

'Do you know Otto Schmidt?' Gordinho nodded his head to show he did. 'He's a friend of mine and, from all accounts, he's in a spot of bother. I came back to Porto Alegre to see if I could do anything to help.'

'Very commendable,' Gordinho said, 'but of absolutely no interest to me.'

This brought us to the point of no return and I drew a deep breath.

'I intend to stay three days anyway,' I told Gordinho. 'If you refuse to play ball we may as well have it out here and now. I don't like to threaten people but I don't seem to have much choice. You're obviously out to get me so it would be no more than self-defence to shoot you.'

It was a weak, unconvincing threat and Gordinho knew

it. He slowly eased his bulk off the bar stool and hitched up his sagging trousers. It could be my hard line had him filling his pants, or it could be he felt the way he looked.

'Shoot me then,' he said before turning his back to begin his stately progress towards his office.

The sound of the shot was monstrously loud, making me jump although I was the one who'd pulled the trigger, and it was a good job I'd had a whole wall to aim at because the Colt's recoil was more powerful than I'd allowed for. Gordinho showed he was human after all by freezing in his tracks, only his weight preventing him from leaping the six feet in the air I would have managed in his place. For a second we were frozen into a tableau, with me watching the smoke eddying from the muzzle of the gun and Gordinho halted in mid-stride, then the babble of noise from the rear of the building broke the spell. Gordinho started walking again and I raised the Colt, knowing damn well that I didn't dare shoot him. Luckily Gordinho wasn't in on the secret.

'You've got your three days, Philis,' Gordinho said without turning his head. 'God help you if you overstay your time.'

The university park wasn't exactly an oasis of beauty. There were more brown patches than grass, the scrubby trees weren't likely to inspire anyone to flights of poetic fancy and the so-called zoo would have given any self-respecting member of the RSPCA epilepsy. The large, artificial lake was the only decent spot, once you ignored the bottles, ice-cream cartons and fag ends wallowing on the surface, and I wandered round it while I tried to assess the implications of the confrontation at the Scirocco.

Stripping away all the gun waving and melodrama I couldn't see where I'd gained much. Natural optimism reminded me that Gordinho had agreed to three days' grace, stark common sense told me I'd promise almost anything to prevent someone putting a bullet into my back. And, once the threat was removed, I'd no longer consider those promises as binding. It was far more likely I'd actually worsened my position—shooting up the club wasn't the kind of action designed to endear me to people.

In any case, worrying wasn't going to help matters. Gordinho would do whatever he felt like doing, his actions completely out of my control. My job was to find Otto and with only three days to manage it in, if that, the sooner I started the better.

As I had plenty of nervous energy to burn I decided to walk to the restaurant, keeping a weather eye open for everything from falling tiles to men in passing cars with machine guns. Otto's place, the Scheherazade, was on the Independencia, a thoroughfare leading directly to the city centre. I'd never discovered whether Otto had done it on purpose but I'd always suspected the name afforded him secret amusement. Not many people could boast of being the German proprietor of a Hungarian restaurant in Brazil which was named after an Arabian princess, especially with all the waiters dressed in gaucho costume. Although this was quite a combination it couldn't obscure the excellence of the food.

When I arrived, warm browed and slightly out of breath after the long haul up the Independencia, it was to find the restaurant virtually deserted. As it was barely half-past eleven this was hardly surprising and I sat myself down in one of the booths with a beer for company. The waiter who served me was new since I'd last been there and the other two I saw briefly on their way to the kitchen hadn't been members of the old staff either. I'd been sitting in my seat for well over half an hour before other customers began to drift in, the vanguard of the lunchtime rush, and it was only then that the man I'd come to see put in an appearance.

It was almost impossible to visualize the Scheherazade without Jair, the head waiter. He was as much an institution as Otto himself and my early morning gloom dispersed as he took his habitual stance in the middle of the floor, an expression of benevolent paternalism on his face. His eyes went straight past me in his initial survey of the clientele and I thought he hadn't recognised me, then they came back and he started towards me, making no effort to hide his pleasure. I stood up to greet him, both of us indulging in a brief session of back slapping before Jair dropped into the seat beside me. The other customers were examining me curiously, wondering who the hell I was to rate such a reception. Friends of Jair automatically became members of a severely restricted élite.

'How long are you here for, Philis?' he asked, beaming all over his podgy face.

'Only three days, just long enough to look everyone up. I came here first to see how you and Otto were.'

At the mention of Otto's name Jair's smile tightened, a wary expression crossing his face. He didn't seem eager to volunteer any information and I wondered why. He must have known he wouldn't be able to hide Otto's disappearance from me.

'Is Otto skulking in the office?' I asked, to help him out. 'Or is he getting lazy in his old age and spending the mornings in bed?'

'He hasn't arrived yet,' Jair answered, his eyes distinctly shifty.

This hedging had me worried, was completely at variance with his usual open nature. If it had been a simple matter of Otto disappearing Jair should have been only too glad to pour out the story to an old friend. Instead he was deliberately being evasive and I had no option except to force him out into the open.

'Cut the crap with me, Jair,' I said bluntly. 'Otto's disappeared hasn't he? You haven't seen hide nor hair of him for a fortnight.'

For a moment Jair just stared at me, pain and sadness etched into every line of his features. Still he wouldn't talk.

'They need me in the kitchen,' he said woodenly, pushing himself to his feet. 'I'm afraid you'll have to excuse me.'

All the while I was eating Jair remained closeted in the kitchen and his attitude bothered me more than anything else that had taken place since Reece had walked into my life. He'd been with Otto since the Scheherazade had opened for business in 1948 and, over the years, he'd become more of a friend than an employee. Moreover his loyalty was unquestionable, something which made his reluctance to talk all the more incomprehensible. There was, of course, the possibility that Otto himself had instructed Jair not to say anything but this couldn't satisfactorily account for the fear I'd seen in his eyes. His behaviour, down to the last gesture, suggested Jair thought it dangerous for him to discuss the disappearance with me. If this was the case it was logical to suppose it was equally dangerous for me to wander around asking leading questions. One way or another it seemed I was well and truly up the creek. And in desperate need of a paddle.

Although the meal was superbly cooked, as all food at the Scheherazade had to be before Jair allowed it out of the kitchen, I failed to do it justice. For all it mattered I could have been eating a jam butty instead of veal gulyas. A nagging voice kept reminding me how easy it would be to pack my bags and take the first flight to Montevideo or Buenos Aires. I listened to it attentively, so attentively I didn't realise Jair had brought my bill until he spoke.

'I hope you enjoyed your meal, Philis,' he said, handing me the platter. 'It's been nice seeing you again.'

Muttering the appropriate words of embarrassed appreciation I paid up and left more hurriedly than was consistent with good manners. Walking down the Independencia was a lot easier than struggling up had been and as I went I pulled the crumpled bill from my pocket. It didn't give the slightest clue as to how much the meal and drinks should have cost but it did tell me Jair would be in the Beethoven Bar at eight that night.

CHAPTER IV

THE BEETHOVEN was on the Farrapos and I arrived there a few minutes early. This was a waste of effort, and I knew it, because lack of punctuality was a Brazilian national characteristic but the place was an old haunt of mine, with a lot of memories attached, and I didn't mind waiting. It was a small bar, the crowded tables cramped closely together, and this helped to give plenty of atmosphere. I found a seat under the large wall bust of the kraut composer, drinking dark beer and Steinhager while I ran an experienced eye over the women, most of them from the city's two universities. It was good to see the standard hadn't dropped, either quantitatively or qualitatively and even the blind pianist was giving them the once over from behind his pebble-lensed dark glasses. They might be the untouchables, girls from good families who were destined to marry intact, but they were still nice to look at.

By nine o'clock I'd given Jair up, not that his failure to show came as a surprise as the day's investigation had made me increasingly pessimistic. So far half of Porto Alegre knew I was trying to find Otto and all I'd learned in return was that no one had the foggiest where he might be. From the Scheherazade I'd made directly for Otto's house where I'd questioned the servants and gone through his personal papers, my search producing exactly nothing. The rest of the afternoon and early evening I'd spent with no greater success, calling on every one of Otto's friends and business acquaintances that I could think of. Everyone professed to be delighted to see me, half of them lying through their teeth, and none of them could provide the slightest lead. Everywhere it was the same story. Yes, they were shocked by Otto's unexpected disappearance, no, they hadn't informed the police or tried to find him them-

60

selves. Not that I'd expected anything else for non-involve-
ment was another facet of the Brazilian creed. Unless Jair
turned up it didn't seem as though I'd be needing the
three days' grace Gordinho might possibly be giving me.

At half-past nine I decided it was pointless hanging
around any longer. Instead I'd do a tour of the clubs,
entirely for my own entertainment, and then to bed, pre-
ferably not alone. I was actually asking for the bill when
Jair came through the door, looking almost blasphemously
informal in the open-necked sports shirt he was wearing, a
complete contrast to his splendid gaucho gear at the
restaurant. He stood there uncertainly for a minute, peering
round the smoky interior of the bar, and he didn't see
me until I waved my arms to attract his attention. He
didn't think of apologising for being the odd hour and a
half late and I didn't take him to task. At least he'd
arrived the same day as he'd specified which was more
than most of his fellow countrymen would have managed.

'Why did we have to go through the cloak and dagger
routine at the Scheherazade?' I asked after I'd set him up
with a beer.

Jair shrugged his shoulders and held out his hands
deprecatingly.

'It would have been dangerous to speak there,' he said
simply. 'It's probably dangerous just meeting you here.'

It was the answer I'd been expecting but this didn't
make the news any more palatable. Even the liberal
amount of schnapps percolating through my system didn't
cheer me up.

'Tell me all about it,' I said, displaying remarkable
sang froid. 'Exactly what has Otto got himself involved
in.'

'I just don't know, Philis, and I haven't the slightest
idea where he is either. I only wish I had.'

'But you do know it's dangerous to talk about his disappearance,' I prompted.

Jair sighed heavily. He wasn't enjoying himself and was
making no attempt to disguise the fact.

61

'I'd better tell you the whole story and let you judge for yourself.' He paused to collect his thoughts. 'A fortnight ago, on the Wednesday, Otto told me he had to go off on a business trip and he wouldn't be in for a couple of days. This was nothing unusual. He often left me in charge for a day or two while he was away and I didn't think anything of it. When he hadn't returned by the Saturday I still wasn't particularly worried. I merely thought he'd bumped into some old flame of his and decided to make a weekend of it. It certainly wouldn't have been the first time this had happened. You know yourself how Otto is with women.'

I nodded confirmation.

'Just carry on with the story.'

'Well, as I said, I wasn't particularly surprised when Otto didn't come to the restaurant on Saturday. Normally he sent a telegram if he was away longer than he'd anticipated but at this time of year the lines into Porto Alegre are down more often than not and the fact he hadn't notified me didn't mean a thing. By Monday, though, I was worried. It was the longest he'd ever been away, apart from holidays, and there was still no word from him. I decided that if I hadn't heard from him by the time we closed I'd have to contact the police. I never had the chance. That night when we were clearing up two men came in. They gathered all the staff together and told us Otto would be away for a long while, several weeks at least. Meanwhile we were to keep the restaurant running as usual and if anyone asked we were to tell them Otto was in the Argentine on holiday. We were also to let them know about anyone who persisted in their enquiries. To show how serious they were they picked out one of the waiters for a demonstration. He's still in hospital.'

'And you let them get away with it?' I asked.

I wasn't condemning Jair in any way. After all, there were certain similarities to the manner in which I'd allowed Gordinho to push me around.

62

'What else was there to do?' Jair said bitterly. 'I owe a lot to Otto but I've a wife and family to think of. Even if I took the risk and went to the police what good would it do? I think Otto is dead.'

I didn't contradict him, the possibility already having occurred to me. What Jair had just told me made it far more of a probability.

'The two men,' I said. 'Did you know them?'

Jair shook his head sadly.

'They were from out of town and I didn't recognise either of them. One was a German, a big man, about your size, with crew-cut hair and a broken nose. The other man was smaller and fatter. The thing I remember about him was the way he smiled all the while they were hitting and kicking poor Ignatio.' Jair shuddered perceptibly. 'That one's a killer, a real sadist.'

They sounded a lovable couple and if I had the misfortune to bump into them I hoped I'd see them first.

'How do you keep in touch with them? Did they give you a phone number or an address?'

'No. Someone rings up the restaurant every morning and I think they must keep an eye on the Scheherazade as well.'

The conversation died a natural death and we sat sipping our drinks. The descriptions were no use at all. I could spend a lifetime in a city the size of Porto Alegre without bumping into either of the two men and my life expectancy there was only a little over two days, if that. Against my better judgement I was committed now, intent on discovering what had happened to Otto, and, to my frustration, all the obvious lines of enquiry appeared to be blocked.

'Did Otto give any indication where he was going?' I asked at last.

This was the question I should have asked first but the answer was so predictable I hadn't bothered. As expected Jair didn't have any more idea than the other people I'd asked.

'He could have gone anywhere,' he told me, disappointed he couldn't be more help. 'The restaurant isn't his only business interest and he was always travelling. Curitiba, Caxias, Rio Grande, Passo Fundo, I could name a dozen places where he had contacts.'

'In that case there's only one way I'm likely to find him,' I said resignedly. 'You said you were supposed to make a report about anyone asking for Otto. Have you told the mystery men I'm looking for him?'

'No, of course not,' Jair retorted indignantly, shocked I'd thought him capable of such perfidy.

Drawing a deep breath I counted slowly up to ten, then I counted to ten again before I committed myself to becoming a hero.

'Make certain you tell them tomorrow,' I instructed Jair. 'Really lay it on thick. Say I don't intend to leave Porto Alegre until I've discovered where Otto is.'

'You're sure,' Jair asked unhappily, not at all struck with the idea. 'Those men are dangerous.'

'I'm absolutely positive,' I said, speaking with far more conviction than I felt.

Jair had to return to the Scheherazade just before eleven and I left the Beethoven shortly after him. Now my neck was well and truly on the line I desperately needed some relaxation. Porto Alegre offered plenty of choice as far as night life was concerned but by now I was in a mood where nothing but the best was good enough. Accordingly I took a taxi out to Melanie's.

The club was a good seven miles from the city centre and well worth every yard of the trip, many people swearing it was the best bordello in South America. I was in no position to confirm this but it was difficult to see where it could be improved upon. Meals weren't served and this was the only reason I hadn't stayed there instead of a hotel for everything else was to hand. The fittings were elegant and comfortable, there was a private beach on the lagoon, the cabaret featured some of the most famous entertainers south of the Amazon and, of course, there were the women, every last one of them hand picked by Melanie who was one of the world's greatest authorities on what was likely to please a man. Just seeing them gathered together under the same roof made a mockery of international beauty contests. This was why Melanie's opening ceremony had attracted every bigwig in the area, from the governor of Rio Grande do Sul to the Police Chief of Porto Alegre, and others from as far as Rio de Janeiro. The place had so much class it made Gordinho's plush Scirocco Club look like a knockshop in the Gorbals.

Inside the club I took a seat at one end of the bar, making sure I wasn't beneath one of the chandeliers, and sipped a cuba libre while I slipped into the atmosphere. This definitely wasn't the kind of establishment where half naked whores rushed around being slapped on the rumps by drunks and, on the surface, it was more decorous than the average W.I. meeting. At the far end of the room a Paraguayan quartet, complete with harp, were on the stage singing a plaintive song about love on the Pampas, watched appreciatively by an audience of fashionably dressed men and women. The only indications to the real nature of the club were the youth and beauty of the women compared with the middle-aged obesity of their escorts. In fact the only two customers on the right side of forty were Reece and myself. He'd come in a minute or two after me and was sitting at one of the tables with a fragile, little Japo-Brazilian. It was obvious he had no intention of acknowledging me but it was nice of him to let me know he was around. What with Reece, and Gordinho's man sitting in his Volkswagen in the car park, I was beginning to feel like the Pied Piper.

Melanie herself, a far from unattractive blonde although she was nearly fifty, was mixing with the customers, supervising operations. After ten minutes or so she spotted me and came unhurriedly across.

'How's God's gift to women?' she asked. 'I'd heard you were back in town.'

'News travels too fast for my liking,' I said, not really surprised.

'It's the price of fame. Anyway, I've been expecting you for a week.'

This did surprise me.

'You have?'

'As soon as I heard about Otto I knew you'd be back,' Melanie told me. 'Gordinho or not you weren't going to sit back quietly in Santos without doing anything to help.'

Melanie broke off the conversation to order a couple of drinks from the barman. Apparently she had a hell of a sight more faith in me than I had myself.

'What progress have you made so far?' she asked once we were both set up.

'None beyond learning that Otto is in real trouble,' I told her. 'The bloody idiot seems to have gone off without telling anyone where he was going.'

Melanie wrinkled her nose in sympathy.

'I know how you must feel. I made a few enquiries myself without getting anywhere.'

I just bet she had. She'd been in love with Otto for years, although I doubt whether he'd realized it, and she wasn't the type to play safe and ignore his disappearance. Otto was the reason I got on so well with her. As his best friend she accepted me automatically.

'Have you seen Lydia?' Melanie asked suddenly.

'Not yet,' I admitted. 'I intended to pop up to Caxias when I had time.'

'Oh, she's not at the Vie en Rose any longer, she moved down to Porto Alegre. I've been meaning to see her myself. She may know where Otto went.'

'How come?' I asked, not following Melanie's line of reasoning.

'Since you left her in the lurch she's been seeing a lot of Otto. They had a lot in common. Otto was like a fish out of water without you for company and Lydia was

66

even worse. If anyone knows where Otto is it should be her.'

I hadn't expected Lydia to be overjoyed to see me and she didn't disappoint me. When she saw who her late-night visitor was she immediately slammed the door in my face, or she would have done if I hadn't foreseen her reaction and had my foot in the way. Nevertheless she did her best to crush all my toe bones before I leaned against the door with my shoulder and pushed it open.

'Get out,' she spat furiously. 'I don't want to see you.'

It was inconceivable she really meant this so I shut the door behind me. Lydia was part Italian, part Brazilian and part Paraguayan, all volatile races in their own right and liable to go off like nitro-glycerine when mixed together. To prove the point she launched herself like a wildcat, prepared to use teeth, nails, elbows or feet just so long as she could hurt me. The most sensible thing would have been to hit her hard on the jaw but ingrained chivalry forbade this and I concentrated on defending myself. I managed to grab her arms before she could gouge out my eyes, jerked my ear out of range of her teeth and held her firmly while she squirmed, struggled and kicked.

'Let me go,' she hissed, her blood really up, 'or I'll scream.'

Both my arms were fully occupied so there was only one way to stop her. For a few seconds she continued to struggle, her lips cold and unresponsive, then her body relaxed against mine, her surrender as absolute as it was sudden. The aftermath of all her tantrums in the past had been a passionate reconciliation, her anger transformed into an almost animal appetite for sex.

'Am I forgiven?' I asked softly when I eventually took my lips from hers and came up for air.

In reply Lydia tilted back her head and treated me to a slow, sexy smile. The invitation in her eyes was transparent and I was about to leer back when she brought up her knee as hard as she possibly could. Unladylike it may have been, painful it certainly was. I screeched out loud, released Lydia and doubled over, clutching myself unashamedly.

'You cocky bastard,' she shouted, picking up a candlestick from the table near the door. 'Thinking you could walk in here after three years and hustle me straight into bed.'

I knew exactly what she intended to do with the candlestick and there was nothing I could do to prevent her. In my doubled-up stance the back of my head made a tempting target and Lydia was in no mood to miss. Being made of wood the candlestick didn't do much damage, not nearly so much as her knee, but I did a nosedive on to the soft part of the carpet, fed up to the teeth with a fight where I couldn't hurt Lydia and she could tear out my heart if she felt like it. Keeping my eyes tightly closed I lay motionless on my face, listening to Lydia's frenzied harangue. Beginning with an initial challenge to stand up and fight she proceeded, via a brief précis of my ancestry, to a detailed exposition of what she thought of any man who treated a woman as badly as I'd treated her. Despite her blatant distortion of the truth I gave no signs of having heard a word and, after five minutes or so, her temper subsided sufficiently for her to realise that when a fully grown man spent this length of time lying on the floor with his eyes closed there might well be something wrong. Especially if he'd just been hit over the head with a blunt instrument. Lydia's monologue ceased, presumably while she worked this out.

'Are you all right, Philis?' she asked tentatively, anxious now.

Answering her wouldn't do my cause any good so I kept quiet. Lydia dropped abruptly to her knees, rolled me over and cradled my head on her lap, her thigh making a much more comfortable pillow than the carpet. Now she thought I had concussion or a fractured skull her anger had completely dispersed, to be replaced by loving concern. In a mixture of Portuguese and Italian she implored me to

68

speak to her, swore she hadn't meant to hurt me and told me how much I meant to her. There was a lot more besides, all of it good for the ego, and I lay back luxuriously, trying not to blink when an occasional tear splashed on my face. Mention of calling a doctor decided me it was high time to begin a protracted recovery. To my mind three would be a crowd. To start the ball rolling I moaned weakly a couple of times, then opened my eyes, my exaggerated grimace intended to signify intense pain.

'What happened?' I whispered, thoroughly enjoying myself apart from a nasty ache in the crotch.

Relief at my return from the dead prevented Lydia from answering me and she remained bent over my reclining body, looking like a weeping Madonna. If I'd ever been asked for a blueprint of my dream woman it would have been a replica of her, from the sheen of her Spanish black hair to the shape of her little toe. She was the only woman I'd proposed marriage to, and the only one who'd turned me down flat. Hers had been the right decision as well. I could have no more settled down to monogamy than she could have resisted knifing me the first time she discovered I'd been with another woman.

'Are you all right, Philis?' she asked brokenly, the tears sparkling in her eyes making them greener than ever. She must have had a drop of Irish blood in her as well.

'I feel great,' I mumbled gallantly. 'Just as if I'd had a shower under the Iguacu Falls.'

Putting on the agony a bit more I tried to struggle to my feet, Lydia helping me up. Leaning heavily on her, with my arm round her waist, I allowed her to lead me through into the bedroom and ease me down on to the bed.

'You'd better stay here tonight,' she said, starting to undo my shirt. 'You're in no fit state to go anywhere else.'

Out of politeness I didn't raise any objection. After all, who was I to argue with a lady?

It was late morning when I awoke. Lydia was still

69

asleep with her head on my shoulder, the coffee cream of her skin putting my tan to shame. Pushing a strand of hair from her face I gently nuzzled her mouth until her eyes opened.

'You look horrible when you snore with your mouth open,' I said romantically.

She bit my nose and sensually moved her body against mine, making my toes tie themselves in knots.

'I don't snore,' she said complacently, running her nails lightly down my spine, 'and I never look horrible.'

It was on the tip of my tongue to ask who'd told her she didn't snore, then I thought better of it. Instead I lowered my head to her breasts, teasing the nipples with my lips and tongue. We made love unhurriedly, neither of us having any need to prove ourselves because we'd done all the proving that was necessary a long time before. When we eventually pulled apart I wondered what was to stop us staying together in bed for the rest of my stay in Porto Alegre. Unfortunately the answer came only too readily to mind.

'Why have you come back to Porto Alegre?' Lydia asked, almost as if she'd read my thoughts. 'Gordinho will kill you if he finds out and, however much I'd like to flatter myself, you wouldn't risk your life just to see me.'

'Too true I wouldn't,' I told her. 'Especially if I'd known how you were going to greet me.'

Lydia laughed and cuddled up against me.

'It was only because I was so pleased to see you. It was such a shock to find you standing at the door.'

'I shudder to think how you'd greet anyone you weren't pleased to see. The way you behaved you'd think it was my fault we hadn't seen each other for three years. You were the one who refused to go to Santos with me, even as my legally wedded wife.'

It was a mistake to mention this. Lydia's temper, never totally quiescent where I was concerned, was beginning to smoulder.

70

'Did you really expect me to after you'd admitted you'd been shacked up with Gordinho's fancy woman?' she flared.

'I wasn't shacked up with her,' I protested. 'I only saw her the once.'

'And how many more times would you have seen her if Gordinho hadn't found out?' Lydia accused, rapidly losing control.

'OK, OK,' I said, deciding it was time to change the subject. Another stand-up row wasn't going to do anyone any good, least of all me. 'Don't let's argue about something that happened three years ago. Just remember that any time you need a husband I've put in my application.'

'Was that a proposal?'

She'd half sat up in bed, looking at me to see if I was serious and restored to her good humour. I hauled her down again.

'Of course it was,' I assured her. 'After all, you can cook, you're house trained and you're not too bad in bed. What more could a man ask for?'

Overwhelmed by my chat Lydia called me querido, I called her nennizinha and bonitissima and we once again indulged in the oldest of indoor sports. I would have married her as well but we both knew the answer was no. Lydia still had to learn she'd make a better wife than a singer and I finally had to realize there wasn't anyone over the hill just that little bit better.

It wasn't until she'd finished cooking us brunch that we again mentioned the reason for my presence in Porto Alegre. Once more Lydia provided the lead.

'Have you seen Otto yet?' she asked. 'He's missed you.'

'How could I have seen him?' I replied, taken aback by her question.

'You mean you came straight here after you arrived?'

There was a pleased expression on Lydia's face and a bemused one on mine. She was talking as though she expected Otto to be at the Scheherazade as usual.

71

'Surely you know he's vanished. If not you're about the only person in town.'

'Vanished?' Lydia echoed.

There was no mistaking the surprise in her voice.

'That's right,' I told her, a sinking sensation in my stomach. 'No one's seen him since a fortnight last Wednesday. That's the reason I came back. I'm trying to find out what's happened to him.'

'I didn't know,' Lydia said, completely taken aback. 'I've had an engagement in Santa Maria for the last two weeks. I didn't return until yesterday.'

'That's that then,' I said bitterly. 'I might as well give up if you've no more idea where he went than anyone else.'

'But I do know where he went,' Lydia broke in excitedly. 'He went to Rio Grande to see a man called Biddencourt. The day before I left for Santa Maria Otto came to see me. When I told him about my engagement at the Florianopolis he said it was a pity I wasn't going to Rio Grande, then we could have travelled together.'

'Which day was this?' I asked, scarcely daring to believe in my change of fortune.

'It was a Tuesday. The day before you say he disappeared.'

Lydia and I took the afternoon flight to Rio Grande. It hadn't been my idea that she should accompany me, in fact I'd protested strongly, but Lydia had refused to be gainsaid. I'd informed her that I wouldn't be returning to Porto Alegre for more than a few hours and this was what had made her so pigheaded. She maintained it was so long since we'd last been together she had no intention of allowing me to disappear again after one night together, especially as she had a week off before her next singing engagement. When I'd brought up the little matter of how dangerous the trip might be, a point I'd really emphasized, she hadn't batted an eyelid, saying Otto was as much her friend as mine. Nor would she agree to the obvious compromise—a trip to Santos after I'd sorted everything out. In the end I'd given in gracefully. It was clear she'd go to Rio Grande whatever I said and she was less likely to get into trouble with me to keep an eye on her.

Before we left for the airport there was a lot of rushing around to be done. First I had to sort out my position at the Hotel Broadway. As an optimist I assumed I'd want to return to Santos from Rio Grande and the only practicable flight plan would involve a change of plane in Porto Alegre, almost certainly meaning a stopover of several hours. The possible alternatives, going through Montevideo or Buenos Aires, would take me out of Brazil. Without a lot more pull than I had in Rio Grande do Sul just getting the exit visa might be a week wasted. After this I'd have to sweat things out for an even longer period, wondering whether I'd be granted a re-entry permit and knowing it was quite on the cards that the Brazilian authorities would decide the country's economic development could progress without me. Accordingly I paid a week in advance for my room at the Broadway, explaining I wasn't absolutely sure when I'd be back. The great advantage was that I could leave the bulk of my luggage behind and take with me nothing more than an overnight bag, a real boon for someone who hated packing as much as I did.

Once this was satisfactorily arranged, a more complicated affair than it would appear thanks to the effusive ineptitude of the staff, I had a couple of phone calls to make. The first was to say cheerio to Gordinho and to mention I'd be passing through Porto Alegre some time in the next few days. The second was to the number Reece had given me, a report on my progress to date. I now knew for certain that the story he'd told me was a pack of lies, ten minutes with a banking acquaintance had told me this, but, whatever the reason, Reece desperately wanted to locate Otto. With a return fare from England, his other travelling and living expenses and the £500 I was being paid he'd made a considerable investment in the search. Moreover the dossier about my past activities could only

73

have been compiled by Otto, a fact which placed him and Reece somewhere on the same side. Until something more definite turned up I accepted Otto's connection with British intelligence, entertained grave doubts about the Nazi fantasy, completely discounted the forging angle, and had an unpleasant premonition about my intended role. It was all too easy to visualize myself as the classic fall guy, the man who stuck his neck out for the axe, while Reece watched complacently from the sidelines, ready to step in when my usefulness was over.

The notion made me feel rather like a sacrificial goat but, seeing Reece on the plane to Rio Grande, another possibility occurred to me. It could be he was sticking so close in order to offer me some protection when things became really sticky, not that the thought provided me with much comfort. Staked-out goats had a notoriously high mortality rate, even with an intrepid white hunter standing by.

On the plane Reece again refused to acknowledge me, although Lydia and I had taken a seat directly across the aisle from him, and I played the game by ignoring him in return. He wasn't my idea of good company anyway.

If the flight through an incipient thunderstorm was rough Rio Grande wasn't a great deal better. It was the place where the word moribund had been invented and, by rights, it should have been established as a penal colony for people who complained about the smog in Los Angeles. Not that there was any smoke, just a miasmic atmosphere of green hides and drying fish. Once upon a time it had been an important port, now it was on the way down and would die completely as soon as someone had the bright idea of constructing a deepwater canal to Porto Alegre. Then ships would no longer have to sail the length of the lagoon before exiting to the open sea at Rio Grande.

Barring some recent additions the town's buildings dated from the opulent period and were now quietly decaying. The hotel Lydia and I booked into was an elaborate late-

Victorian affair, sinking fast by the looks of it, and, to judge by our reception, we might have been the first paying guests for a month. We were shown to an enormous room with an exotic view of the port installations, prompting me to pull the curtains, but at least the bed was comfortable. I forgot about Biddencourt for the day and, with Lydia's willing assistance, I gave the bed a more thorough testing.

Next morning I woke up early, regretting this immediately I discovered Rio Grande's unique stench hadn't diminished over night. It definitely wasn't the kind of town where people flung wide the windows and did deep breathing exercises, not unless they were suicidally inclined, so I rang down for breakfast. When this arrived I wished I'd taken my chances at the window. The coffee tasted as though it had been prepared at a sewage farm, the fruit was over ripe and the bread was stale enough to have been salvaged from the Ark. After we'd showered and dressed it seemed a wise precaution to drink a Fogo de Sao Paulo apiece in the bar downstairs, just to sterilize our stomachs.

Lydia didn't keep me company for long. She wanted to visit a friend doing cabaret at one of the local clubs and left me fooling around in the bar, filling in time until I could decently call on Biddencourt. Although there was nothing to suggest he'd had anything to do with Otto's disappearance I had a totally illogical foreboding about the man. Over the second glass of the green firewater the feeling became so strong I debated whether to take my gun visiting with me and even went so far as to return to my room before common sense took over. The threatened thunderstorm still hadn't broken and the lowering humidity made wearing a jacket and carrying several pounds of hardware about as tempting as a hair shirt. Laughing at my faintheartedness I threw my jacket back on to the bed, the gun in a side pocket. Assuming the very worst Biddencourt was hardly likely to become violent merely because I asked a few questions about Otto.

At first glance Biddencourt's establishment didn't strike me as a thriving concern. The wooden fence surrounding it badly needed a new coat of paint, the big, double gates sagged dispiritedly on their hinges and the yard inside was littered with piles of empty fish boxes, many of them in a bad state of repair. To add to the general effect the odour of rotting fish was exceptional, even by Rio Grande standards.

It didn't take long to appreciate the place wasn't exactly a hive of industry. A rapid census detailed myself, several evil-looking cats and an emaciated Negro, wearing a tattered pair of swimming shorts which might once have been blue beneath the accumulated filth. The Negro was meandering between the piles of boxes, pushing a broom ahead of him in a manner which suggested he was too weak to bear the full weight rather than any serious intention of cleaning up. He looked up as I came in, then continued with whatever he was doing. I moved in amongst the boxes to head him off, kicking hissing alley cats out of the way and trying not to plaster pieces of fish heads all over my shoes.

'I'm looking for Senhor Biddencourt,' I said as he bore down on me.

The Negro dug in his heels, stopped, leaned on his broom and breathed out heavily. I took an involuntary step backwards as the cachaca blast withered the hairs in my nostrils, doing my best not to gag too noticeably. To judge by the liquor haze surrounding him he would have blown a large chunk of southern Brazil into mid-Atlantic if he'd tried to light a cigarette.

'Can you tell me where to find him?'

He seemed to be having difficulty sorting out the implications of my original tentative approach. My question apparently merited serious consideration. The sweeper knitted his greying brows, slipped a hand into the top of his shorts for an intimate scratch, hawked deep in his throat and effortlessly shot a gob of yellowish phlegm twenty feet over his left shoulder. I had to jam my hands in my pockets to stop myself from clapping.

'He's in the office,' he articulated slowly once the performance was over. Either he had a speech impediment or the cane spirit had paralysed his tongue.

Considering his duty done he pushed past me and continued his erratic course. Left to my own devices I looked around me, unable to see anything remotely resembling an office.

'Where is the office?' I shouted after the retreating figure.

Reluctant to stop again once he'd built up momentum the Negro made a vague gesture with his thumb as he went on his way, stalked by a pack of cats. Interpreting his directions I made for the enormous warehouse which was nothing more than a corrugated iron roof held up by haphazardly placed wooden pillars. After five minutes spent working my way through the boxes I struck lucky, spotting a small, brick building in one corner of the warehouse.

The interior came as a pleasant surprise, a striking contrast to the squalid chaos outside. Biddencourt might not be interested in providing an elegant front for his business but he certainly believed in looking after his creature comforts. The air-conditioning hummed placidly, the fitted carpet was so thick I was in danger of bogging down and all the furniture was that year's model. The secretary manicuring her nails behind the desk was any year's model, a dark mulatto housed in the kind of body which should have been put on permanent display. To give her a treat I flashed her my sexiest leer.

'Go straight in, he's not busy,' she said briefly before returning her attention to her nails.

Slightly piqued by the casual way she'd dismissed me I went through the door into the main office. The furnishings were up to the standards established by the secretary's cubby hole, the crowning glory a huge, leather-topped desk, far too large for the room which contained it. Biddencourt was sitting behind the desk, busily doing nothing. He

77

was another Negro, a surprising thing for a successful businessman to be south of Rio de Janeiro, and his immaculate suit would have put many a Wall Street executive to shame.

In keeping with his appearance he was far too refined to ask who I was and what I wanted, lifting his eyebrows in polite enquiry instead. People had done this to me before, mainly at school, and I'd never liked the habit so I let him hold the expression until he started to go bug-eyed, giving the impression of having just realised there was a tarantula in his underpants.

'My name is Philis,' I told him before his eyes popped out and spoilt the desk. 'It won't mean anything to you but I'm hoping you can help me. I'm trying to trace a friend of mine.'

Biddencourt shunted all movable facial features around, endeavouring to express concern, surprise and willingness to help at the same time. It was a great performance and, uninvited, I plumped down in a chair opposite him.

'Who is it you're looking for?' he asked.

His voice was beautifully modulated, the Portuguese as perfect as any you'd hear in the Copacabana Palace. In fact his exterior was so smooth I suspected he spent hours each day practising in front of a mirror.

'Otto Schmidt,' I said bluntly. 'He left Porto Alegre just over a fortnight ago and no one has seen or heard of him since.' I paused for a minute to allow Biddencourt to manipulate his face into the extreme surprise position. 'I know he was coming to Rio Grande to see you and I was wondering whether you had any idea where he went from here.'

'You mean Otto has disappeared?' Biddencourt breathed in disbelief.

As everything else about him was so phoney it was impossible to tell whether his amazement was genuine or not. Not seeing why I should waste my voice acting as a foil to his histrionics I nodded my confirmation. Biddencourt leaned back in his chair, fingers steepled under his chin to convey thought, widened his eyes as he reached a decision and bent briskly forward to flick through his desk diary. When he came to the entry he wanted he lifted his head to give me a man to man look.

'Naturally I'd like to do everything in my power to help clear up the mystery,' he announced. 'Apart from being a valued customer Otto is a dear friend of mine. Unfortunately I'm as much in the dark as you appear to be. He came to see me on the twenty-third but what he did or intended to do after he left me I just don't know. He comes to Rio Grande six or seven times a year so the visit didn't strike me as anything out of the ordinary. I assumed he would be going back to Porto Alegre once his business here was finished. From what you say I gather he didn't.' Biddencourt shrugged his shoulders. 'I'm sorry but I'm afraid that's all I can tell you.'

'Did you notice anything unusual about his behaviour?' I asked for the sake of form.

'Nothing I'm afraid.'

Biddencourt's tone was final and it seemed I'd reached another vital point of decision—I could either accept the brick wall blocking my search or try to probe a bit further. The latter alternative appealed to me most. Having gone this far I was stubbornly determined not to give up until I had exhausted every possibility and I had a sneaking suspicion Biddencourt knew more than he cared to admit. I didn't like his punctilious use of the present tense when talking about Otto, I didn't like his lack of curiosity and, come to that, I just didn't like Biddencourt. It was time for a calculated risk.

'How well do you know Otto?' I asked.

'We've been doing business together for several years,' Biddencourt answered, wondering what I was leading up to.

'That means you must know him fairly well,' I mused. 'Have you heard any rumours that Otto wasn't primarily interested in the Scheherazade? That it's really a front.'

This time there was no mistaking Biddencourt's surprise,

or his new sense of caution.

'Rio Grande is a long way from Porto Alegre,' he said. 'It's quite possible Otto has business interests I'm not aware of.'

'I wasn't thinking in terms of business,' I told him. 'I've been out of touch with Otto for three years and over the last day or two I've asked a lot of people if they had any idea what might have happened to him. One man I saw told me something which sounded pretty far-fetched at the time. Now it's beginning to make as much sense as anything else does. He said Otto has been attached to British intelligence since he came to Brazil and that he came to Rio Grande in this capacity. I realize this sounds ridiculous but at least it's a possibility.'

The barb went home and Biddencourt was rocking for a second before he managed to force a laugh. It gathered conviction the more he practised it but it was still distinctly hollow. I laughed with him for a while and then I left. Mighty oaks were supposed to grow from some seeds. What, if anything, was going to grow out of mine God only knew.

CHAPTER V

ONE THING was clear after my interview with Biddencourt —Lydia and I definitely had to part company. It had been madness allowing her to accompany me in the first place, now she was leaving even if I had to carry her on board the plane. Back in Porto Alegre Jair should have passed on the message I'd left with him and in Rio Grande I'd gone a step further, as good as telling Biddencourt I knew far more about Otto than was healthy for anyone connected with his disappearance.

There had never been any doubt in my mind about the trouble Otto had to be in, the probability being that he was already dead, and I was deliberately asking for trouble from the same source, the one sure way of following his trail. Admittedly Reece was lurking in the background, a potential guardian angel, but I had nowhere near enough faith in him to want Lydia in the firing line if my suspicions about Biddencourt proved to be correct. She had to leave Rio Grande and I had to stay, prepared for disaster just as I had been since Reece had entered my life.

When I reached the hotel the room key was still on its hook and Lydia hadn't returned by the time I'd knocked back a much-needed whisky in the bar. Getting drunk didn't seem to be a good idea so I wrenched myself away and took the lift up to my room. The man seated in one of the chairs, a chubby, little mulatto, was a stranger, not to mention being a hell of a surprise. The smile he bestowed on me as he rose did ring a bell, though. There were millions of smiling Brazilians apart from the one Jair had told me about, they filled all the travel posters, but none of the others had any reason to be in my room.

Purposefully I advanced into the room, switching on my nastiest grin to show how pleased I was to make his acquaintance, so intent on my appointed victim that I forgot about the big, broken-nosed German who travelled around with him. Until he kicked the door shut behind me, that is. I swung round fast, hands cocked for immediate action, leaving my stomach beautifully exposed to the rock hard fist approaching it at mach-2. If I'd had a chance to tense my stomach muscles the German might have broken every bone in his hand, though I doubt it. As it was my navel was transformed into a small crater, pieces of intestine wrapped themselves round my backbone and I rolled on the floor, groaning ecstatically.

'You can call me Lutz,' the German said generously. 'My friend's name is Joao. We'd both prefer it if you didn't make a fuss.'

'I'll be as silent as the grave,' I said, forcing the wit out through clenched teeth.

I was still in my foetus position on the floor, waiting for

the pain to sink to agony level and wondering how I could reach my jacket which was still lying on the bed, apparently undisturbed.

'You can get up now.'

To go with the instructions Joao kicked me in the kidneys. I made a big production out of rising from the carpet, doubled over and groaning until I was half-way up, then I straightened suddenly and swung wildly at the German's jaw. I didn't get anywhere near him, of course, and I was already rolling in anticipation of the counter. Even so it was a hell of a good punch and the side somersault I performed on my way across the room definitely wasn't intended. Largely because of this I didn't manage to land on top of the bed, crashing into the side instead, but I did succeed in grabbing the tail of my jacket as I fell, dragging it down beneath me. Although my brain might be in working order the two punches had done me a power of no good, making my fingers as nimble as untrained bananas when I endeavoured to free the gun from the folds of cloth, my body a shield to conceal what I was doing.

'That wasn't very sensible,' Lutz said in gentle reproof.

The nasty ache on the right hand side of my jaw told me he wasn't far wrong, especially as the Colt seemed to be hopelessly snagged. On the spot I vowed to file off the useless front sight if I ever had the chance.

'What do you want?' I mumbled, looking at the intruders over my shoulder and stalling for time.

They were standing by the door, both of them supremely confident. Lutz was massaging his bruised knuckles and Joao was playing with a knife. It was Joao who answered me.

'You'll find out soon enough,' he said. 'First of all you're going to tidy yourself up, then we're going for a drive.'

He was halfway through when the gun came loose, by the time he'd finished I had thumbed back the hammer and was rolling on to my back.

'Sorry boys,' I said, my good humour restored. 'Mother

told me never to accept lifts from strangers.'

Joao was frozen into compliant rigidity, impressed either by my simple, homespun philosophy or by the gun, but Lutz didn't display the respect I'd anticipated. He should have done because his hand was still snaking towards his left shoulder when the bullet struck him, hurling him back against the wall. There was plenty of time to swing back the Colt and take aim at Joao before he had a hope of escaping through the door. His back made a lovely target and it would have been all too easy to shoot him if there'd been any sense in such an action. There wasn't so I didn't pull the trigger. I hadn't wanted to kill either of them, just ask a few pertinent questions, and one body in the room was problem enough without becoming a mass murderer.

Even from where I was lying there could be no doubt Lutz was dead. The entry wound in the middle of his forehead was small and clean, the mixture of blood, brains and bone messing up the wallpaper suggested it was a different story at the back. Stifling my repugnance I went across to him, knowing there wasn't a great deal of time to set the scene for crowds materialized from nowhere in Brazil and a variety of sounds were already converging on my room. Lutz had his gun in a shoulder holster and, trying not to look at his head, I pulled it out, a handkerchief wrapped round my hand. When the first of the curious arrived, a hotel porter, I was still bending over the corpse but the gun was lying by Lutz's right hand. The porter won by a short head from a gaggle of three or four other competitors, all of them stopping in the doorway to gawp at the gory tableau.

'Robbers,' I gasped, still doubled over, my gun in one hand and the other clamped over my bruised diaphragm. 'They tried to rob me.'

The performance taxed my acting ability to its limits. To avoid further explanations I stumbled across to a chair. With my head in my hands, apparently overwhelmed by the events of the last few minutes, I was in a position to ignore the babble of speculation and start dreaming up a story which would get me off the hook.

After five minutes or so a 100 decibel increase in noise signified the advent of the police, three of the vanguard posting themselves round my chair. I was busily maintaining my air of bemused shock, not all of it assumed, but this was completely wasted. There were soon at least twenty policemen crowded into the room, both uniformed and in plain clothes, and the result was indescribable chaos. In fact, if I hadn't been so intimately involved, I would probably have laughed. Scores of instructions were being hurled out and instantly countermanded, one group of plain-clothes men was on the verge of blows and the room was so full there was scarcely space for the body.

Gradually, however, a chain of command was established and a semblance of order created. An official photographer, who behaved as though he was a refugee from the Italian press, took shots of Lutz from every conceivable angle, plus a few which weren't. A couple of men appeared with a collapsible stretcher, threw Lutz on to it and carted him away, leaving only a chalked outline of the body and a lot of blood behind them. Eventually they were so well organized someone remembered they had the killer in the bag already.

At once I became the focus of attention, half a dozen detectives gathering round to bombard me with questions, most of them totally irrelevant. There were so many of them trying to horn in on the act they didn't even manage to set up any of the elementary traps policemen seemed to delight in, not that I would have contradicted myself in any case. Everything I told them was gospel truth, although I did neglect to inform them of a few salient facts and I might have misled them a trifle by saying Joao and Lutz's intent had been robbery pure and simple. With these minor exceptions I was a veritable George Washington, hammering home the point I'd killed only in defence of life and property. Loath as they were to believe me I was getting the message across after about an hour and a half. Nevertheless, when the police began a mass exodus they asked me to accompany them.

My departure from the hotel in the middle of a tight police cordon bore some resemblance to a royal progress. The corridor was lined with curious spectators and the foyer downstairs was absolutely packed, flash-bulbs popping frantically and even a small television crew on the scene. The police phalanx forced its way to the exit, one or two senior officers peeling off to give their exclusive interviews, and hustled me down the steps to the waiting line of cars. Mine was at the head of the queue, motor already idling and the driver at the wheel, completely incurious behind his shades. Ungentle hands pushed me into the back seat, a policeman squeezed in on either side and we were away before the rear doors had banged shut, leaving all the hullabaloo behind.

Sinking back as comfortably as I could in the crowded conditions I tried to unwind, although there was no great rush. No court, not even a Brazilian one, was likely to convict me for killing Lutz but there was the dilatory police procedure to go through and, quite probably, considerable delay before the inquest. However much I paid to grease the wheels of justice there would be no question of departing from Rio Grande until the matter had been cleared up.

My immediate preoccupation was with how I could contact Lydia and Reece so it was a moment or two before I realized the policeman on my right was digging me in the ribs. Seconds later I registered the fact he had his gun pressed into my side and I turned to him in surprise.

'Just sit still and behave yourself,' he said, undisguised menace in his voice.

Taken aback, I wondered what on earth he was talking about. Apart from the inconvenience I didn't have a great deal to worry over and it was in my own best interests to co-operate with the police. Either the man was trigger happy or he'd been watching too many bad movies.

'Try not to kill him,' the driver broke in. 'The boss wants to ask him some questions.'

The voice was familiar, one I'd heard less than two hours earlier, and a quick glance confirmed the identification. For all his police uniform and dark glasses the driver was indisputably Joao, the man I'd so charitably refrained from shooting at the hotel.

Despite the small icebergs in my veins I was unable to suppress a sneaking admiration for Joao, and presumably Biddencourt. In under two hours they'd not only managed to acquire three police uniforms from God knew where but cooked up a plan which had whisked me away from two dozen genuine policemen with hundreds of civilians looking on. This made the second occasion in a matter of days that I'd been taken for a ride by bogus policemen and, of the two, Joao's masquerade was so professional it put Reece's amateur theatricals completely in the shade. The measure of its brilliance was that although I'd been the central character I didn't have the slightest idea how I'd been spirited out of official hands.

Nor did I discover how the getaway was effected. Once the suburbs of Rio Grande had fallen behind us I sat unprotesting under the threat of the gun while the man on my left picked a spot with clinical detachment and tapped it with his riot stick.

I came round to the carolling of birds and a nasty pain in the head. Tactile examination proved there was no dent in my skull, just a big lump behind my left ear, but it had been some tap, my watch showing it was now the middle of the afternoon. Some time during the period of unconsciousness I'd arrived wherever it was Joao had been instructed to bring me and, judging by the accommodation, I wasn't regarded as an honoured guest. In fact the room was specifically designed to aggravate my claustrophobic tendencies—bare walls, high ceiling, solid door and small, barred window. The furniture wasn't out of Ideal Home either, affording me no aesthetic pleasure

86

whatsoever. The carpet, for want of a better name, was worn down to its jute backing, no hint of its former pattern remaining, the small, lopsided table was made of a close relation to plywood and an all wooden chair had been put together from a child's do-it-yourself kit by someone unable to follow the instructions. And, finally, there was the bed, a sagging, iron-framed monstrosity which might have been the ultimate in comfort back in the Dark Ages but which definitely wasn't meant for twentieth century man. I knew because I was the twentieth-century man lying on it.

Even my throbbing head didn't tempt me to stay on the lumpy mattress. The antique washbasin in one corner hadn't struck me as particularly decorative, now I discovered it wasn't functional. My first attempt to turn the solitary, rusty tap failed to budge it an inch and repeated efforts were no more successful. This left the window as my only entertainment. There was a lovely view if you liked hills and trees and the rest of the nature scene and it was cool enough to suggest the house was several hundred feet above sea level. Personally I preferred streets and people and neon signs to being held prisoner in the foothills behind Pelotas which was where I had to be. The area didn't exactly rank with the Yangtze basin as a centre of population, averaging about one peasant to the square mile, and I couldn't see the one in my sector doing anything to rescue me. This left Reece and, knowing how unfrequented the roads were in the region, I didn't rate his chances of having done a successful tail job very highly, not unless he doubled as the Invisible Man or had a helicopter in his suitcase. This assumed he'd been in position outside the hotel when I'd been snatched.

One way or another the prospect didn't make me want to leap for joy. Being a prisoner wasn't my favourite pastime and screaming got on my nerves, especially when it was a woman screaming. It began as I turned away from the window, a full-blooded affair expressing everything a scream normally did—terror, revulsion, pain. Every hair

87

on my head bristled for the three minutes the shrieks lasted, then they tailed off into gurgling sobs and I went back to the bed to think about the kind of people who could make a woman scream like that. This did nothing at all for my morale.

No one tried to make me scream until eight o'clock in the evening and before then I had one or two surprises, none of them pleasant. I'd been in the room for four hours when Joao and another man, a shrivelled-up, little Brazilian Indian who answered to the name of Pepe, came to fetch me. Regardless of claustrophobia I wasn't overjoyed to see them. The only reason I hadn't been killed was that someone wanted to ask me some questions and I had an uncomfortable premonition I didn't know enough of the answers to satisfy my interrogators, let alone myself. Nor did Joao's behaviour bolster my confidence.

'Shift your arse,' he said.

At least that's what he might have said if he'd been an American citizen. Portuguese was a much more colourful language.

In my book two guns to none constituted overwhelming force and I allowed them to hustle me out of the room. There was a long, dark corridor outside, flanked by closed doors and with a flight of stairs half-way along. When I reached the top of the stairs I looked back over my shoulder, wondering whether I was supposed to descend.

Apparently I was. Joao placed a hand in the small of my back, then pushed, sending me base over apex, bouncing painfully from stair to stair until I reached the stone-flagged floor at the bottom. Physical injuries were negligible, nothing more than a few bruises to keep my headache company, but the gales of laughter from Joao and Pepe as they came down by more conventional means made me see red. I stayed on the floor, gritting my teeth and hoping one of them would come close enough for me to demonstrate my own sense of humour. This meant Joao had a chance to kick me in the side, just as he had earlier in the day, and I didn't mind a bit. It merely showed he hadn't learned from experience.

Groggily I scrambled to my feet, lurched towards Joao as I rose half upright and did something to him no gentleman should do to another. Joao was the only one upset by the breach of etiquette and his mouth was opening on a bellow of pain when I fitted the heel of my left hand under his chin and heaved. His teeth clicked together again, his feet left the ground and he was still airborne as the door on the far side of the passage burst open from the impact of his body.

Pepe either had slow reflexes or he was under strict orders not to shoot me. Whatever the reason he dithered helplessly while I knocked aside his gun and did my honest best to punch his head through the wall. Although I didn't even dent the plaster Pepe's eyeballs were rolling up as he slid to the floor and I headed towards the nearest exit. This was the moment Biddencourt chose to put a bullet into the fleshy part of my right thigh.

'You really are a silly man, Philis,' he said indulgently, standing in the doorway I'd just thrown Joao through.

It was the kind of remark he could afford to make from behind a loaded gun and I treated it with the contempt it deserved, reserving my attention for my wounded limb. Although it had suffered little more than a deep scratch I regarded all parts of my body as vital, hating to see any of my quota of blood trickling away, and I used a strip torn from the tail of my shirt to bandage my thigh. Only then did I spare Biddencourt some attention.

'You should be more careful,' I reproved, striving for the light touch although I wasn't feeling at all humorous. 'You might have done me a serious injury.'

'Don't worry, I probably shall,' Biddencourt comforted. 'If you're quite ready you'd better come in here.'

He obviously relished his new role as the smooth, master criminal, finding this a pleasant relief from being the suave, super-efficient executive. Suppressing the suspicion that Biddencourt might not be acting this time I did as he suggested, limping through into what proved to be a kitchen. Through the leaded windows I caught a glimpse of a yard and outbuildings which showed the place had once been a farmhouse, then Joao distracted my attention, slamming the barrel of his gun against my cheekbone. It wasn't much of an effort as he still had one hand cradling his crotch and I didn't find it too difficult to stay on my feet. Just the same I wasn't sorry when Biddencourt stepped between us to push Joao back.

'Don't be impatient,' Biddencourt said. 'You'll have plenty of opportunities to amuse yourself later.' There was a brief pause while he fixed Joao with what was presumably supposed to be a gimlet eye. 'You'd better go to see how Pepe is.'

Joao wasn't noticeably happy about not getting to knock me around some more but he followed instructions and left the kitchen, slightly hunched over and muttering under his breath. For my part I massaged my cheek, wondering whether the swelling was likely to add to my already distinguished looks, and took as much weight as possible on my left leg. I also watched Biddencourt back to the table where he picked up a slim booklet and threw it across to me. Effortlessly I plucked it out of the air, demonstrating what a great close fielder England was in danger of losing.

'Take a good look at it,' Biddencourt suggested. 'It should interest you.'

He was right. Counting the way I'd been pushed downstairs as the first unpleasant surprise and a bullet in the leg as the second, then this made the third of the evening and it was by far the worst. Subconsciously I'd placed a lot of reliance on Reece's help, even though I'd realised it would have taken a near miracle for him to have followed me to the farmhouse, so it was a body blow to finally appreciate I was on my own. I'd been frightened since my arrival in Porto Alegre, a controlled, reasonable fear which had increased the more I'd probed into Otto's disappearance, but now was the time for me to be scared stiff. It wasn't a booklet Biddencourt had tossed to me, it was the same passport I'd examined in Santos a few days before.

Since then there had been considerable changes in its appearance. The photograph of Reece was now disfigured by the black-edged hole which went all the way through the passport and the stained cover was tacky to the touch. There was no need for a forensic scientist to tell me the hole had been made by a bullet or that the stain was blood, meaning another of the imponderables had been swept from the board. Admittedly I wasn't a great deal wiser as a result but at least I knew survival was going to depend on my efforts alone.

When I threw back the passport Biddencourt made no attempt to catch it. As he was obviously expecting me to make some comment I kept quiet, turning to watch Joao and Pepe come into the kitchen instead. Although Joao was walking tall again Pepe was nowhere near to a full recovery from having his head made into a sandwich between my fist and the wall.

'You haven't anything to say then?' Biddencourt asked, snapping my attention back to him.

'About what?'

'Stop playing the fool,' he snarled, his composure crumbling momentarily. 'I was referring to the passport and you know it.'

'Oh that,' I said airily, my nonchalance entirely assumed. 'Depending on which pocket Reece was carrying it in I'd say he's either dead, severely wounded or sitting uncomfortably.'

Biddencourt was quick to seize on my mistake.

'You recognised the name?'

'No,' I answered, more than equal to the challenge. 'I read it from the passport.'

'He's lying,' Joao said from behind me.

The venom in his voice indicated he was still feeling sore and this reminded me that standing around wasn't doing my leg any good. There was a straight-backed chair by the table so I made use of it before replying to Joao's accusation.

'I realize it's probably a shock to you,' I told him once I was comfortable, 'but it's one of my many accomplishments. I've been reading since I was nineteen.'

My attempts to lighten the atmosphere weren't appreciated. For a start, on Biddencourt's orders, Joao lashed me to the chair, binding my wrists so tightly behind my back I thought my shoulders would come out of their sockets. This did nothing to shake my faith in the attitude I was adopting.

'Let's start again,' Biddencourt said menacingly, doing his best to look and sound like a modern Al Capone. 'However clever you think you are you're going to answer my questions one way or another. Joao is quite an expert at persuading people to talk and I'm sure he'd welcome the chance to practise on you. Is that clear?'

'Perfectly,' I assured him, 'but before I begin my life story I'd like you to satisfy my curiosity on one point.'

Predictably, Biddencourt raised his eyebrows in quizzical interrogation.

'What do you want to know?'

'Is Otto dead?' I enquired.

'He is,' Biddencourt answered, his tone bland. 'As a matter of fact he died in the very same chair you're in now. He didn't want to answer my questions either and Joao had to use those powers of persuasion I was telling you about. Unfortunately Joao was a trifle over enthusiastic. Either that or Otto had a weak heart.'

The euphemism slayed me, confirmation of Otto's death not coming as a surprise but adding fuel to my mounting anger. It was Biddencourt's attitude which really got through to me, his smug complacency as he talked about having Otto tortured to death. He was so confident that he was immune from retribution that I just had to show him how wrong he was. Mentally I encased myself into a shell where only three things mattered—survival, escape and settling accounts with Biddencourt. For the first time in my life I had a worthwhile ambition.

Unaware of the fate I was busily dreaming up for him

Biddencourt had taken Joao aside and was whispering in his ear. After a few seconds Joao left the kitchen while Biddencourt came back to stand in front of me. Pepe was still over by the window, shaking his head muzzily. Deliberately Biddencourt brought out a cigarette from a platinum case and lit it with what had to be a gold-plated lighter.

'Of course, your case is rather different from Otto's,' he said meditatively. 'This time I know most of the answers before I put the questions. I merely need your confirmation on a few points. What's more, despite my earlier threats, I don't think I shall have to use physical coercion to make you co-operate. You see I've another prisoner as well as you.'

I kept my face expressionless, helped in this by the advance warning the screaming had given me. Nevertheless it required every vestige of control to keep my voice steady when I spoke.

'Who is it?' I asked, although I'd long since known the answer. 'I hadn't realized I was only part of the collection.'

'If you wait a minute you'll be able to see for yourself,' Biddencourt answered.

The bastard was really enjoying himself, loving the way he could manipulate other people's lives with a flick of his little finger, but I had to hand him one thing. Whatever his other faults Biddencourt was certainly thorough.

Footsteps were coming down the stairs and it was a physical strain to turn my head slowly as Joao brought Lydia into the kitchen. I daren't look Lydia in the eye, only glancing briefly in her direction before I returned my gaze to Biddencourt. Just the same I'd taken in her dishevelled hair, the purpling bruise on her cheek and her torn clothes. All of a sudden breathing was no longer automatic but something to learn anew, my throat feeling swollen to twice its normal size. There was no question of my being able to speak.

'Take a good look at her,' Biddencourt ordered.

Numbly I did as I was told, struggling to keep my face impassive. For her part Lydia was standing like a zombie, half leaning against Joao who had one hand inside her dress, her blank, glazed eyes showing she was in a state of shock.

'You pick your girl-friends well,' Joao said, broadening his smile. 'She was a bit stand-offish at first but Pepe and me soon made her see things our way.'

'That's right,' Pepe concurred from the window, the first time I'd heard him speak. 'She'd do anything for us now.'

Carefully I swivelled my head to face him.

'That's what whores are for,' I said, forcing the words out. 'They provide a service.'

Lydia gasped behind me and I was glad I couldn't see her expression. If she wasn't in shock already she would be soon.

'She's nothing more than a whore to you?' Biddencourt asked. Although he was off-balance he didn't believe me.

'We had a business arrangement,' I lied pleasantly, feeling like a latter-day Judas. Some day I might be able to explain to Lydia that it was for her own good.

'Bring the woman over here,' Biddencourt told Joao, keeping his eyes on me.

Quickly I ran through the list of instructions to the various parts of my body. Eyes indifferent, hands deliberately unclenched, breathing slow and regular, this was the way I was going to stay, whatever happened to Lydia in the next few minutes. Joao was holding her arms behind her, grinning at me over her shoulder, a grin he'd pay dearly for if I had any say in the matter. Biddencourt gripped the front of Lydia's already ripped dress and tugged downwards so Lydia was naked to the waist, her terrified, shallow breathing making her breasts heave. Her eyes were alive again, flashing a mute appeal which I daren't respond to, and I lowered my gaze.

There was an inch of cigarette left in Biddencourt's hand and he delicately tapped off the ash before he ground it on Lydia's shoulder, his eyes not leaving mine for a moment, not even after she started screaming and tried to wrench herself free from Joao's grip. He kept the cigarette pressed against her until there was the faint, sweet smell of burning flesh in the air and all the while I stared at the strained sinews of Lydia's throat, trying to eliminate awareness of her screams. When Biddencourt removed the cigarette he left behind a red, blistered area the size of a shilling and Lydia was slumped forward, her screams converted to hysterical tears.

Anger and sympathy weren't emotions I could afford for the time being and I did my best to push them into my subconscious, saving them for future reference. It was far more important Biddencourt shouldn't realize what I'd been thinking, not until the time came when I wasn't tied to a chair. He'd lit another cigarette and looked rather despondent about my lack of response. According to his book I should have been heaping outraged, hysterical abuse on his head instead of sitting passive and unperturbed. At least, this was the way I hoped I appeared to him.

'Personally, I prefer an ashtray,' I said, striving to reinforce my pose of cynical unconcern. 'I find it's far less wearing on the nerves.'

The slight shake in my voice and the nervous flicker of my left eyelid were perfectly permissible. To Biddencourt they should indicate fear, nothing more, and I was the only one to know they were the outward manifestations of inner storm. During the few seconds the burning cigarette end had been held against Lydia's skin I'd learned a lot about myself. I was an emotional man after all. Anger, compassion, love, they'd all come easily to me and, above all, hatred, an all-consuming lust to drown the memory of Lydia's screams with those of the men responsible. But my brain remained remote and untouched, ticking over like one of IBM's top computers. What had happened, why it had been done, what I could do about it, these were questions to be shelved. The first priority was to keep us both alive.

CHAPTER VI

BIDDENCOURT exhaled smoke through his nose, a glint of what could have been respect in his eyes.

'You're a cold-blooded bastard,' he said, the pot calling the kettle black. 'You really don't give a damn what happens to the woman.'

'Don't let me fool you,' I told him. 'You've persuaded me it would be wiser to talk than have you mess around with her any more. Just ask away. I'll give the answers.'

To fill out the new, amenable image I gave Biddencourt a big, open smile which cost me two or three days' calories to produce. He didn't believe me any more than he was intended to.

'Tell me about Reece,' he said softly.

'Well, I did meet him the once,' I admitted. 'It was on the plane from Porto Alegre to Rio Grande. He was sitting directly across the aisle from me.'

'This was the only occasion you met?' Biddencourt queried.

I nodded confirmation, radiating patent dishonesty.

'What did you talk about?'

'I can give you our conversation verbatim,' I said obligingly. 'I said, "Would you like to borrow my paper bag?" Reece just said, "Aaaooouugh," then he rushed off to the lavatory. It was a very rough flight.'

A smothered snigger from the window showed Pepe couldn't be all bad but the language Joao used did nothing to revise my opinion of him. Of the three Biddencourt was by far the most impressive. All he did was smile tightly and tap the ash from his second cigarette of the session.

'Please, Philis,' Lydia implored, her voice hysterical as she anticipated the next move. 'Tell him what he wants to know.'

This direct appeal came closer to breaking through my

defences than the screams had done earlier and I had to bite my tongue to hold back as Biddencourt leaned forwards. Lydia flinched and began to struggle, Joao gripped her tighter and pulled her elbows further back, Pepe moved away from the window for a better view, and I tried to stop my teeth from grinding. An inch from Lydia's nipple the cigarette halted.

'Take her back to her room, Joao,' Biddencourt said, withdrawing the cigarette. 'We're not going to get anywhere this way.'

A wave of relief swept over me and I began breathing again. The first round was definitely mine, with Lydia temporarily removed from the firing line, but I shuddered to think what this had cost. It had always been a gamble, not least because once I'd convinced Biddencourt that Lydia meant nothing to me beyond a good lay there was no reason he shouldn't have killed her straight away. Unsavoury as the thought was, I hadn't expected them to kill a woman as attractive as Lydia until it was essential, probably not until they disposed of me, and, as events had turned out, I'd been vindicated. Now it was up to me to ensure we weren't killed for a long, long while.

The essence of torture, as I understood it, was that it should be tailored to individual needs, as much psychological as it was physical. Biddencourt, however, held total disdain for finesse, placing all his faith in acute, physical pain. This technique had probably worked with Otto and he could see no reason why it shouldn't have the same results with me. Unfortunately, from Biddencourt's point of view, he wasn't to know I didn't have nearly so many of the answers as he expected.

Quite early on, before there was any real need to tell the truth, I let Biddencourt know everything about Reece's visit to Santos and how I'd been blackmailed into working for him. My aim was to present him with the entire truth as I knew it, to tell it in such a manner he'd think I was lying and had a great deal more to tell. I had to create the impression of concealing something from him, to establish myself as someone too valuable to kill. Admittedly, this line meant I was going to be badly hurt, tortured for information I didn't have but this was a hell of a sight better than Lydia and myself being dead. Or so I hoped.

As Biddencourt had suggested Joao was cast in the role of torturer in chief, with Pepe as his faithful Indian assistant. First, however, Biddencourt used the cigarette originally destined for Lydia, stubbing it out on my wrist. This was exceedingly painful and I had no inhibitions about screaming. Perhaps some people would have sat and suffered the injury without a wince but, to my mind, they'd be absolute idiots, just asking to have something worse done to them. To go along with the screams this was when I babbled out everything I knew. After my apparent indifference to Lydia's maltreatment the capitulation was far too sudden and Biddencourt didn't believe a word I said. This meant it was all over bar the shouting and that was all going to come from me, together with gasps, groans, shrieks and anything else I could think of to express my feelings.

Three hours was an awfully long while to have people doing the kinds of things which were done to me, deliberately designed to break my will, and, if I'd had anything left to tell, Biddencourt would have learned it in half the the time. Before any further questions were asked there was the softening-up process, Pepe steadying the chair while Joao worked me over, calmly, methodically and impersonally. There was a lot of blood on his hands by the time he'd finished and, as all of it had come from my nose and mouth, I was glad there wasn't a mirror handy. Not that it would have been much use because my eyes had ceased to focus properly.

Then came the questions, going on and on, interspersed with various indignities inflicted on my person. Mainly Biddencourt wanted to know about Otto, Reece and a man called Pawson, my answers invariably proving to be unsatisfactory. At first I was in agony but gradually, almost imperceptibly, the pain eased and I slipped into a dreamy half-world where nothing really mattered until, eventually, it was someone else being tortured while the real me floated above, watching dispassionately. It must have been about then that I first lost consciousness.

Immediately I came round properly I wished I'd postponed the awakening for a year or two, pain signals flashing in from all parts of my body, arriving so fast it took me a minute to interpret them all. My face was closest to the sorting office in my brain so it received priority. I still didn't have a mirror handy but my features didn't feel like part of the old head I used to take around with me to grow hair on. This new face was a swollen, misshapen monstrosity, extremely tender to the touch and with a nasty taste of dried blood in the mouth where one of the teeth had been removed. Farther down was my body, minus a lot of skin where Joao had practised some fancy knife work, decorated with the odd cigarette burn and, worst of all, a lot of bruising where my kidneys had been patted with a rubber truncheon. The sum total of these injuries was a lot of pain I could well have done without but, on the credit side, all my limbs could be moved and seemed to bend only in the appropriate places. This was important. I was going to hurt whether I lay still or hobbled around and I preferred to hurt while I escaped from the farmhouse.

For the time being I wasn't going anywhere. The fact that Lydia was still a prisoner lent urgency to the situation but other considerations came first. I needed a chance to recuperate, to work out the routine of the house and, above all, to find a way out. In any case, there was no immediate danger, of this I was sure. When Biddencourt had finally called a halt to Joao and Pepe's exertions I'd been in a bad state after repeated submersions in the sink. The three of them had been talking while I lay in my own, personal pool of water on the flagstones, only vaguely aware of the voices above me. Nevertheless, my subconscious had grabbed hold of one snatch of conversation, replaying it again and again until I woke up on the bed. Gordinho's name had been mentioned several times, and in a manner which proved he was the man in charge, the person ultimately responsible for my present predicament, something which seemed eminently logical now I thought about it. I still didn't know what Reece had mixed me up in, only that this had nothing to do with the British Treasury, but it was obviously something important and Gordinho had a happy knack of popping up wherever big money was concerned. His involvement also accounted for several things which had puzzled me, especially the reason why I'd been left unmolested in Porto Alegre. This had had nothing to do with my gun play at the Scirocco Club, Gordinho had merely wanted to discover my exact connection with the Otto before he took any drastic steps against me. And it was to Gordinho I owed my life, temporarily at least, not to my own cleverness. Lydia and I were alive simply because Biddencourt didn't dare kill us without Gordinho's prior authorization.

The main obstacle to escape wasn't my physical condition or the locked door but the three men left to guard Lydia and myself. Although Biddencourt and Pepe had departed, presumably to confer with Gordinho, Joao had been reinforced by the two men I'd last seen in police uniform. Three armed men would take a lot of getting past, the odds against me far too high for my liking, but I couldn't afford to delay action for too long. By midday I decided I'd waited long enough, that my gaolers were less of a threat than the prospect of an execution order from Gordinho, and I was actually examining the door when I had the piece of good fortune I so richly deserved.

The sound of a car engine starting up wasn't world shattering in itself but it had me over to the window in a flash, in time to see the Kombi bouncing away from the farmhouse with two men aboard. Rapid calculation on my fingers told me that two from three left one, a far more satisfactory state of affairs as far as I was concerned. I had no means of forecasting how long the Kombi would be away, probably not for any appreciable length of time, but I hoped I'd have enough time to deal with the remaining guard.

To achieve this I had to escape from the room and there were plenty of clever ways of doing it. I could have tried to dislodge the bars across the window, for instance, but they were set in solid concrete and I didn't have a fortnight to spare. The same went for tearing up the floorboards or chipping through the walls. As a reasonably civilised member of society I was accustomed to using doors and I could see no good reason for changing the habits of a lifetime. Not unless I had to, that is.

Just the same I had no illusions about the outcome of an attempt to entice my guard into the room. A spot of quiet lock picking was called for and the simple, mortice lock was child's play for someone who'd spent his adolescence at a mixed boarding school. The contents of my pockets had been removed but I didn't have to look far for tools, only as far as the bed in fact. Beneath the mattress the base of the bed was a wire mesh of springs, tightly coiled springs about eight inches long which hooked on to one another. The wire was a trifle thick for my liking and it took me a good quarter of an hour to straighten half of one of the springs, leaving the rest for a handle. The lock itself required less than five minutes to deal with, then I had to lock the door again. There were bolts on the outside and, without a hacksaw, there was absolutely nothing I could do about them.

This disposed of the easiest way out, now I had to use my ingenuity. Removing one of my shoes I began to hammer at the door, shouting at the top of my voice. I soon had a sore throat and an aching arm but there was some consolation. The noise had Joao rushing upstairs like a bat out of hell, mightily displeased at being disturbed. Indeed, some of the epithets he was using as he approached the room were enough to make me blush.

'Stop that row,' he bellowed as he reached the door.

'Otherwise I'll fix you so you can't make any noise.'

For a brief moment I was tempted to take him up on the offer, then common sense prevailed.

'Isn't it about time I had something to eat and drink,' I asked through the peephole. 'I haven't had anything since yesterday morning.'

Joao laughed unpleasantly.

'There's no sense in feeding dead men,' he told me. 'Just keep quiet and save your strength. You'll need it when the boss gets here.'

Still chuckling, he went back along the corridor, cheered on his way by the choice obscenities I shouted after him. Although Joao was the kind of person everyone should hurl abuse at there was no particular malice behind the words. I hadn't expected him to provide me with a seven-course meal, or even with bread and water, I'd just wanted him to pay his visit at my convenience, not while I was busy breaking through the ceiling.

Unless the house had three stories, which seemed un-likely, my room should be directly underneath the loft. Or attic, as the case might be. Semantics apart, this was an important distinction. Where I came from the loft was the bit left over at the top of a house, the gap between the roof and the ceilings of the top floor rooms. An attic was a room utilising this space and, in common with most rooms, it had a floor. Shifting floorboards in the time available was beyond me so I had to hope for a loft with nothing but lath boards and plaster between the beams. If not I'd have to think again.

Standing on the low bed alone was no go, this wasn't high enough for my purposes. The mattress made a far from stable base and the table was rickety in its own right but after three abortive attempts I found I could more or less balance on it in a kneeling position. Satisfied, I clambered down and turned my attention to the chair. This was a marginally sturdier piece of furniture than the table, far better suited to being knelt on, but even with plaster and lath board I wasn't going to shout Shazaan and stick my fist through. Instead I broke off one of the legs, minimizing noise as much as possible. The nails sticking out at the end made it ideal for working on the ceiling and, as a second string, I fancied the prospect of batting Joao around with it.

Although the ceiling didn't prove to be much of a barrier my precarious perch didn't help matters a great deal. Nor did my dented skull, battered face, and cigarette-burned, semi-skinned torso, not to mention the bullet graze on my thigh and the fact I hadn't eaten for an eternity. Luckily I had all the heroic qualities and a little discomfort wasn't going to stop me, especially when I thought of what was likely to happen if I was still a prisoner after Gordinho decided my fate. Ignoring the shooting pains in my kidneys I chipped steadily at the plaster, careful not to allow any of the bits and pieces to clatter to the floor. Once the first small hole had been made it was easy work and in no time at all I had opened a gap between the beams large enough to pull myself through.

So far, so good. I sat on one of the beams, my legs dangling through the hole, and worked out where I would have built the trap if I'd been the architect. My eyes were no use to me because it was almost pitch dark in the loft, with only a chink of light here and there to indicate a loose tile, and the fetid smell arising from generations of accumulated rodent's crap didn't encourage me to linger long. Moving cautiously from beam to beam I made for where the trap ought to be, keeping the rats and mice at bay with muttered imprecations whenever a stray splinter dug into my knees or hands. As a navigator I was absolutely brilliant, finding the trap exactly where I'd expected to—above the small landing at the head of the stairs.

Of course the bloody thing had to be locked, secured by a bolt or padlock on the other side. If I'd had the time I would have pushed out a few tiles and exited via the roof but this wasn't on. Someone had just started up the stairs, Joao unless his two friends had returned without me hearing them, and although he could be going any-where on the upper floor I couldn't take the risk of him paying a visit to my ex-cell. The trap looked flimsy enough and I was sufficiently battered already for a little more suffering not to make much difference so I closed my eyes and jumped.

It was rather like being hung without a rope but I couldn't have timed my leap better with a NASA type countdown. An unsuspecting Joao was two steps from the top of the stairs when I materialized through the ceiling in a storm of splinters and the shock must have been so great it was a wonder he didn't die on the spot of a heart failure. To even things up I landed off-balance, jarring my already damaged kidneys, something which spoiled my aim with the chair leg, only catching Joao a glancing blow before we both fell backwards.

Joao had the whole flight of stairs to tumble down, find-ing it just as uncomfortable a process as I had the previous night, and I was hobbling down after him, the chair leg gripped firmly in both hands, while he was still on the floor. Joao's mistake was to bank on the knife in his pocket instead of trying to retrieve the gun he'd left on the kitchen table. His greatest asset, my relative lack of mobility, was wasted while he fumbled in his pocket, enabling me to reach the bottom step as the knife came free. It was no use to him at all. I swung the chair leg baseball fashion, the whole weight of my body behind the blow, and the crack when I connected was so loud I thought it had broken in two. Joao's heartfelt screech of pain, plus the drunken way his right hand dangled at the end of his arm, told me otherwise. What I did then wasn't pretty or gentlemanly and it wasn't intended to be. By the time I'd finished one end of the chair leg was sticky with blood, the geography of Joao's face substantially altered, and I'd enjoyed administering the beating. Philis was beginning to strike back.

Before I broke the glad news to Lydia there were several

other matters to attend to, notably the two men who were likely to return at any moment. I could have tried to take Lydia to safety before their arrival but this would have entailed striking across country on foot and I preferred to drive away in the Kombi. Until the Kombi was in my undisputed possession Lydia was far safer locked in her room. Also it would be silly to raise her hopes and then get myself killed.

Although Joao wasn't likely to be very active for an hour or so he was far too dear to me to take chances with. Dragging him by his greasy hair I hauled him through into the kitchen, a fitting setting for what might well follow. What with Otto, myself and now Joao there'd soon be a mock-up of the place in the Chamber of Horrors. The gun I was looking for, a lousy Nacional, was lying on the table and this went into my pocket, Joao taking its place. The blood-stiffened rope which had bound me the previous night was in a corner of the room and I made good use of it, strapping Joao in a modified crucifix position across the table top. I also went through his pockets. His wallet was no treasure trove, yielding three blurred photographs, an inconsequential letter and the cruzeiro equivalent of five pounds, a disappointingly small amount. Morale wise the most important discovery was a couple of packets of Continental, Brazil's most popular cigarette.

With a cigarette drooping sluttishly from one corner of my mouth and the Nacional in my hand I went out of the kitchen, not into the hall but outside into the early afternoon sun. Down in Porto Alegre or Rio Grande it would have been blazing hot, a powerful inducement to stay indoors with a long, iced drink close to hand, up in the hills the edge was gone from the temperature. Normally I was no nature lover, restricting my rural rambles to short hikes from one open air bar to another. Now, after the hours cooped up in the farmhouse, it was a genuine pleasure to be outside gulping carbon monoxide free air into my lungs, listening to the chirruping of cicadas or whatever and surrounded by trees I couldn't identify.

The house and outbuildings were situated at the end of a small valley. On three sides they were bordered by gently sloping, wooded hills while on the fourth a rutted track led, presumably, to civilisation. The pain in my back precluded the climb up one of the slopes for a more general survey so I contented myself with a superficial examination of the two outbuildings.

One of them, probably built at the same time as the farmhouse, was a wooden affair, its earth-covered roof sagging dangerously. Originally it must have been a stable or cow shed but, over the years, it had deteriorated into a playground for rats, lizards and whatever other creepy crawlies infested the area.

The second, a brick construction, was far more modern, only two or three years old at the outside. Its interior was far more interesting as well, confirming something which, to my mind, had always been on the cards. Reece, God rest his soul, had definitely been conning me about the forging. Unless banknotes could be made from coca leaves, that is.

Although I'd always steered clear of drug peddling myself there wasn't a great deal I didn't know about the Brazilian market. Two great, cash drug crops grew wild in Brazil. The most widely spread was cannabis sativa which sprouted up like a weed all over the place, quite apart from the farms where it was carefully cultivated. In Santos hash was dirt cheap and a packet of reefers cost little more than ordinary cigarettes in England. They were smoked quite openly in the streets and bars, with little fear of prosecution, and the number of users in the country as a whole probably ran into hundreds of thousands. This took care of the soft drug market.

For the hard stuff you had the shrub Erythroxylon Coca, now rarely found in its wild state but intensively cultivated in the foothills of the Andes, near to the Peruvian border. By all accounts the indigenous Indian population had been using the stuff since time immemorial, simply chewing the leaves. For sophisticated palates this wasn't good enough, especially as the average addict wouldn't appreciate a trip to the headwaters of the Amazon whenever he needed a fresh fix. Compared with what had to be done to convert raw opium into heroin, processing the leaves into cocaine was relatively simple. Once you had your coca leaves all you needed was hot water, lead acetate, soda, ether, hydrochloric acid, plus a couple of other ingredients I couldn't remember, and you were in the cocaine business. Not that it could be made in the bath. Some rudimentary laboratory equipment was needed, but not a lot as I could see for myself. At a rough guess Biddencourt only performed the end process in his laboratory, having the cocaine roughly crystallized in the north to make for easier shipment.

I was still rooting around in the laboratory when I heard the sound of a car engine in the distance, either indicating one of the neighbours was making a social call or that Joao's two friends were about to return. Once the laboratory was closed behind me I ran hastily to the farmhouse, only to find Joao was still dead to the world and in no condition to shout out a warning. Satisfied on this score I leaned against the wall behind the angle of the kitchen door, waiting for his friends to arrive.

If the two men had been sensible and both come into the farmhouse together they might have lived for while I was now playing by Gordinho and Biddencourt's rules I bore neither of them any particular ill will. Their connection with Biddencourt and the knock on my head one of them had administered I was prepared to overlook, their escape in the Kombi was something I couldn't possibly allow.

The reason for their little expedition had apparently been to pick up some supplies and this was also the reason they didn't arrive together in the kitchen. The man in the passenger seat had gathered up his share of the packages and was on his way towards me, whistling tunelessly as he approached, while the driver was still rummaging in the back of the van. I allowed him two paces into the kitchen before I stepped out from behind the door, the gun jammed into his ribs and one finger to my lips. He hesitated for a second, his arms full of packages, his eyes switching nervously from me to Joao's battered body on the table, then he mistakenly decided to be a hero.

'Look out, Roberto,' he shouted, turning to run.

These were the last words he ever spoke. A fraction of a second before he shouted I'd realized what he intended to do and had tried to transfer the Nacional from his ribs to the back of his head in time to prevent him warning the other man. This was a mistake, on a par with allowing Joao to escape from my hotel room in Rio Grande. I was not only far too slow but I hit him far too hard, the nasty crunch as the gun smashed against his skull telling me I might just as well have shot him in the first place.

He went down with dreadful finality, landing in a mess of broken eggs and milk, and I hurdled his body on the way outside, yet again not moving quite fast enough. The second man, Roberto, had already dropped his parcels and was frantically scrabbling at the door handle of the Kombi but the bullet I fired at his back changed his mind, sending him scurrying round to the far side of the van for cover. Having left the protection of the farmhouse I had no choice but to keep on running, the fifty yards separating me from the Kombi seeming like as many miles.

Roberto didn't waste much time once he had the bulk of the van between us. The first shot came when I'd covered little more than half the distance, the second and third following close on its heels, all of them near enough to indicate the law of averages was in Roberto's favour, especially as the range was rapidly decreasing. This realization prompted me to cover the last few yards in a desperate, sliding dive which ended when I smacked into the side of the van, leaving me at ground level with a beautiful view of Roberto's feet and shins less than ten feet away. Without hesitation I pumped a bullet into the nearest shin, before there was any opportunity for the limb to be moved.

There was an anguished scream, then the rest of Roberto's body joined his feet on the ground and I put a second bullet through the top of his head. He might already have been crippled for life but he'd still had a gun in his hand and I was taking no more chances.

Once I'd checked to make sure the Kombi was undamaged and had dragged Roberto into the kitchen I trudged upstairs, wondering how Lydia would greet me. On the last occasion I'd seen her I'd sat apparently unmoved while a cigarette had been stubbed out on her and had cheerfully informed everyone present that she was a whore. I hoped I'd be able to explain the necessity for this to her but, after what she must have been through, I could hardly expect to find her at her most reasonable. Even so I was totally unprepared for her reaction. From her earlier screams I knew approximately where her room should be and the first door I tried proved to be the correct one. As I unlocked the door with a key from the bunch which had been in Joao's possession Lydia began whimpering inside, a horrible, inhuman sound like a dog anticipating a beating.

'It's all right, Lydia,' I said reassuringly as I went in. 'You're safe now.'

The whimpering continued unabated. She was crouched naked on the bed, her back pressed against the wall as though she hoped to force her way through the bricks, but physically she didn't appear to have suffered further external injury. The cigarette burn on her shoulder flushed angrily and her bruised cheek was badly swollen, otherwise she seemed unmarked. Nevertheless she remained huddled on the bed, wide open eyes staring at me with horror and loathing.

'It's me, Philis,' I said gently. 'No one is going to hurt you.'

To go with the reassurance I'd taken a step towards the bed and this time I got through to her, the whimpering ceasing although she made no move towards me. She

109

allowed me to sit on the bed beside her without objection, but even so her condition worried me. Lydia had aged overnight, her face a pallid, shrunken mask and her eyes seemed to have sunk back into her head, the pupils dilated. The hand I held was cold and clammy to the touch, her breathing was shallow and slow and when I took her pulse it was very, very weak. I didn't need a medical diploma to realize she was in a state of extreme shock.

CHAPTER VII

WHEN I WENT downstairs again I was in a nasty mood. So far Biddencourt and company had had plenty of opportunity to show how rough they could play, now I intended to prove that anything they did I could do better. For the moment, however, Lydia was my primary concern. I'd left her on the bed, wrapped in every blanket I'd been able to lay hands on, and I intended to do what little else I could for her before I had my heart to heart chat with Joao.

Evidently I must have hit him a lot harder than I'd thought because he was still unconscious when I returned to the kitchen, his breathing as healthy as could be expected from someone with a broken nose. Once I'd brewed a pot of coffee I returned to Lydia and managed to force three heavily sweetened cups of this down her throat, the limit of my medical usefulness. Whether or not the coffee did her any good was a moot point but when I left her Lydia was asleep and her breathing seemed to be easier.

In the kitchen Joao was showing no immediate signs of waking up so, to fill in time, I set about patching myself up, making the best use I could of a rudimentary medicine chest I found in one of the cupboards. There wasn't a great deal I could do for my face beyond dabbing disinfectant on the various cuts and bruises, a treatment which did little to improve my appearance. My lips remained distinctly negroid, my nose stayed three times larger than usual and my features retained the general appearance of belonging to someone who'd just boxed thirty rounds with Cassius Clay. The burns were a different matter and I plastered the best part of a jar of Vaseline over them before winding a couple of miles of bandages round my trunk. This didn't do much to improve the way I was feeling but at least it was a step in the right direction.

Joao came round while I was consuming a king-sized ham sandwich although he still didn't look particularly healthy, something I could bear with total equanimity. Provided he answered my questions he was at perfect liberty to peg out at any time he felt like it. After I'd washed down the sandwich with the last of the coffee I pulled my chair over to the table.

'Let's have a little chat,' I suggested.

To give him his due Joao was no coward for, although he was in considerable pain, he did try to make the gesture of spitting in my face. His mouth was too dry for him to succeed but I thumped him in the face to teach him some manners.

'I'll try again,' I told him. 'How long will it be before Biddencourt and Gordinho return?'

Joao said something extremely unpleasant so I punched him again, harder this time, then poked the barrel of the Nacional into his right ear.

'Much as I admire loyalty I don't intend to waste time persuading you to be co-operative. You have exactly ten seconds to answer my question. After that I'm going to clean the wax out of your ears with a bullet. Think it over.'

This wasn't a bluff and Joao knew it. He was well aware I'd almost certainly kill him whether he talked or not but, like any other man, he wanted to postpone the moment for as long as possible. At the count of eight I clicked back the hammer and this was when Joao's nerve broke. He'd had eight long seconds to visualize the bullet cruising through his cranium and the prospect failed to appeal to him.

'They'll be back in about a week,' he said reluctantly.

'You still have two seconds to explain why they'll be away for so long,' I informed him without removing the gun.

'They've gone to Santos,' Joao explained quickly, sensing I didn't believe him. 'They're going to ship out all the cocaine they have in stock, then lie low for two or three months while they completely overhaul the organization. You and your friends have them worried.'

'You're trying to tell me the cocaine is shipped out through Santos?'

Once again I made no effort to mask the disbelief in my voice. Santos was my adopted town, the dock area was my centre of operations and smuggling was my business yet I'd never heard of any significant traffic in cocaine. Belem was the cocaine port.

'That's right,' Joao affirmed, desperate to convince me. 'Gordinho is very security conscious. He thought it safer to have the operation dispersed.'

'How often have Biddencourt and Gordinho been to Santos before?' I asked, slipping in the trick question. 'Do they supervise every shipment?'

Joao started to shake his head, stopping almost immediately, his face contorted with a grimace of pain.

'Neither of them have been there before,' he said once he'd recovered. 'As I said, there are special circumstances. This is the biggest shipment so far.'

Thoughtfully I took the gun away from Joao's head, reluctantly conceding that what he'd told me made sense. The huge volume of trade at Santos would make the smuggling of drugs child's play, could also account for my not having heard rumours about its existence, and it would be far faster than shipping direct from Rio Grande, with the added advantage of being a long way from base. The only snag was the immense distance involved, the thousands of miles from the Amazon down to Rio Grande and then back to Santos. Normally prohibitive transport costs would have made the undertaking financially unsound, even allowing for the fantastic profit margin on cocaine, but this problem disappeared for someone who had a controlling interest in an airline connecting every major Brazilian city, someone like Gordinho, for example. If Joao had told me Gordinho had visited Santos at any time in the period I'd been a resident there I would have known he was lying. As it was I suspected he was telling me the truth.

'There are just two more things I need to know,' I said. 'Whereabouts in Santos can I find Biddencourt and Gordinho and how is the cocaine taken out of the country?'

Nervously Joao licked his bruised lips.

'The cocaine is concealed in bags of coffee,' he told me. 'It travels on a British ship, the *Arcadia*.'

I nodded my head in recognition. The *Arcadia* wasn't a ship I'd had dealings with but I did know it was on a regular run between Santos and Liverpool.

'And where do I find your bosses?'

'I don't know,' Joao replied, fear in his eyes.

As a reward the gun went back to his ear and I treated him to a disbelieving glare.

'It's true,' he protested desperately. 'I swear it's the truth.'

It wasn't worth my trouble to press the point. Santos was home ground and if the men I was after were there I'd have no trouble in finding them.

'I don't know why but I've decided to believe you,' I told Joao, rising to my feet.

'What about me?' Joao asked, his voice unsteady because he already knew the answer.

My answering smile wasn't designed to reassure him.

'I answered all your questions,' he persevered.

'That's right,' I agreed. 'You're no use to me any more.'

I shot Joao twice, the two bullets striking him in the chest before he could start pleading for his life. Shooting a bound, defenceless man wasn't something I could ever be

113

proud of but it wasn't likely to cause me many sleepless nights. All my insomnia would come from thinking about what had been done to Lydia.

People suffering from shock should be kept nice and warm in bed, not ferried around the countryside in a van, but the circumstances surrounding Lydia's case precluded a conventional approach. Dressing her didn't take me very long as there wasn't much to dress her in and Lydia was co-operation itself. She didn't have a tail to wag, otherwise she behaved with the utmost obedience, and this broke me up more than any of my previous experiences at the farmhouse. Violent emotion was something I'd always associated with Lydia, lapdog behaviour was completely alien to her nature.

'Wait here,' I told her once she was bedded down in the back of the Kombi. 'I won't be long.'

She gave no sign of acknowledgement but she made no move to follow when I left, placidly content to remain in her warm cocoon of blankets. With me I took one of the two cans of petrol in the back of the vehicle. Half of it I sloshed around in the laboratory, the rest went into the kitchen. Before I'd driven the Kombi out of sight of the farmhouse flames were already shooting through the wide open windows.

Although the nearest hospitals were in Pelotas or Rio Grande I headed for Porto Alegre, a good six or seven hours away, my decision based on two considerations. The first was the certainty that any delay in delivering Lydia to hospital would be more than balanced by the superior treatment she was likely to receive in Porto Alegre, the second was more personal. Not having seen any newspapers I couldn't tell what the public reaction had been to my disappearance en route to Rio Grande jail the previous day but common sense told me it was a town to avoid, that the police chief there might relish having my head mounted above his mantelpiece as a trophy. I already had enough troubles without venturing into the lion's den.

The major factor working against my crusade to stay out of police hands was the paucity of good roads in the province of Rio Grande do Sul. Without any road maps to assist me I was committed to the main road between Rio Grande and Porto Alegre, an obvious highway for the authorities to concentrate upon. I had to hope they thought I was motivated solely by the desire to escape. This should place the main search towards the Uruguayan border in the south, the traditional route for fugitives, be they criminal or political.

Whatever the actual police dispositions, luck was with us and I wasn't halted once on the long, tiring drive. It took me half an hour to work out exactly where I was, after this it was merely a question of by-passing Pelotas and driving along the sun-baked roads. For her part Lydia lay inert in the back, completely unaware of the passing countryside and perfectly content to leave all the decisions in my hands.

Callous as the thought undoubtedly was, there was no escaping the fact that she was a major liability, as well as being a hell of a responsibility. My problem was I couldn't just walk into a hospital with a woman bearing unmistakable marks of assault and rape, then expect to stroll out again without questions being asked, especially in view of my own state. There were always policemen loitering around the larger hospitals and, in my disreputable condition, it was more than likely I'd be picked up for questioning, even without my Rio Grande notoriety to fall back on. On the other hand I had no intention of entrusting Lydia to the tender mercies of the trainee doctors at a small Pronto Socorro. Stories about them were legion and I, personally, knew of one man who had been treated for pyorrhoea, losing half his teeth before an X-ray disclosed a hairline fracture of the jaw. This might be great training for would-be doctors but it wasn't so good for patients suffering from anything more complicated than a head-ache.

Darkness had fallen before we reached the outskirts of Porto Alegre and when we ran into Novo Hamborgo, one of the satellite towns ringing the city, my mind was made up. In a back street I parked outside a quiet bar, braved the inquisitive stares of the handful of customers inside and placed a phone call.

'Hallo. Who is it?'

Melanie's voice was far from friendly. She disliked being interrupted during business hours.

'It's Philis,' I informed her.

A pregnant pause ensued, surprisingly shattered by Melanie's peal of laughter.

'Public enemy number one himself,' she spluttered. 'I suppose you know every policeman in the state is looking for you.'

'I thought they might be. That's why I need your help.'

'Sorry,' Melanie said firmly, giving me no chance to explain. 'In my business I can't afford to become involved with your kind of trouble.'

'Hold on a second, Melanie,' I protested. 'I thought Otto was a friend of yours.'

With mention of Otto I had Melanie hooked and it didn't take her long to assess the implications.

'Was the man you killed in Rio Grande connected with Otto's disappearance?' she asked.

'He was.'

'And what's happened to Otto?'

'He's been murdered,' I said bluntly. This was a brutal way of breaking the news to her but I didn't have time to lead up to it gently. By now the other people in the bar were whispering together in between shooting suspicious glances at me. 'I can't tell you more over the phone. The important thing is that Lydia's with me and she's hurt. Badly. She has to get to hospital quickly and for obvious reasons . . .'

'How soon can you be at the club?' Melanie broke in.

'In about three quarters of an hour,' I decided after a moment's calculation.

'Park outside in the road. You have got transport, haven't you?'

'Yes. A blue and cream Kombi.'

'Good. I'll be waiting when you arrive.'

There was a decisive click of the receiver at Melanie's end. I had to hand it to her—once her mind was made up she didn't waste time on idle chatter.

It was nearer to an hour later when I drew up outside the club's driveway. Instantly Melanie emerged from the shadow of the hedge, before I'd even switched off the motor, and slid into the front seat beside me. Lydia lay in the back, paying no attention to the new arrival, but Melanie was far from tranquil. There weren't many things she hadn't seen or experienced but the double blow she'd suffered —first the news of Otto's death, now the shock of seeing Lydia's condition—broke through her defences. I was no comfort to her, it was as much as I could do to keep myself under control, let alone shoulder another emotional burden. She had to sort things out for herself, the same way I'd had to.

Tersely I gave her the bones of my story and, when I parked a couple of hundred yards away from the hospital, Melanie had regained a measure of composure. Like me, she had a well-compartmented mind. However great the hurt she could absorb it, rationalize and tuck it away for future reference while she went on with the business of day-to-day living. Crying was for times when there was nothing more important to do.

'How will you handle things at the hospital?' I asked, hoping to assist her return to practicality.

'It should be simple,' Melanie answered, gaining strength with every minute. 'I shall say Lydia is a friend of mine, which is true, and that I found her wandering like this outside the club. Even if the police know she was with you in Rio Grande I've sufficient pull to stop them challenging the story.'

I nodded in agreement. This was far from being a watertight or particularly convincing story but it was a hell of a sight better than anything I could have managed on my own.

'Before I go, though,' Melanie continued, delving in her outsize handbag, 'I brought along a couple of things I thought you might need.'

The tiny, pearl-handled pistol was superfluous and unlikely to stop a charging mouse at a greater range than six feet, the wad of money she pressed into my hand was a different matter altogether. I shoved both gifts into the glove compartment before turning back to Melanie.

'Thanks, Melanie,' I said quietly, underplaying my gratitude because no words could express it adequately. 'I'll cable the money to you from Santos.'

'Don't be silly, Philis,' Melanie replied brusquely, a catch in her voice. 'And don't worry too much about Lydia. I'll look after her. Just make sure you catch the bastards responsible.'

Watching Melanie half carry Lydia into the hospital I felt as if someone had just removed the Eiffel Tower from my shoulders. With Lydia delivered into safe hands I'd returned to a situation I relished, the kind where my sole responsibility was to myself.

The first priority was clothes but simply going into a shop to buy some in the morning was out of the question. The attention my bizarre, battered appearance had attracted while I'd been phoning Melanie had warned me against unnecessary exposure, especially as my photograph must have figured prominently in the local newspapers. Nor did I fancy the risks involved in stealing some. A substantial part of my wardrobe should still repose in room 609 at the Hotel Broadway, together with my spare shaving gear and a fully equipped bathroom. With a convenient fire-escape leading past the window the set-up was too tempting to pass by. The police, of course, would have been through the room but I'd paid for a week in advance and they wouldn't have been authorized to remove any of my possessions. Whatever I might be accused or suspected of, so far I hadn't been convicted of any crime.

Nevertheless, I didn't go in blind, preferring to drive slowly past the front of the hotel before I committed myself. There was no sign of police outside or in the foyer and this was all the encouragement I needed. With the Kombi safely parked in a side street behind the hotel I made my devious way to the back yard. The fire-escape was of the type where the last section was counter balanced, theoretically designed to prevent its use for felonious purposes, and it took me all of thirty seconds to prove how effective a deterrent this was.

For half an hour I really indulged myself, soaking neck high in the bath until I felt up to gingerly scraping the thick stubble from my face and putting on some clean clothes. The bed looked the epitome of comfort, a real temptation, but, reluctantly, I decided this would be carrying audacity too far. It was far safer to drive out of town before I rested. A few hours' sleep, then I'd travel up into Santa Caterina state and catch a bus to Sao Paulo. From there Santos was little more than an hour's drive away.

It all seemed so easy until, a flight down the fire-escape, luck completely deserted me. One minute I was padding quietly downwards in the sheltering darkness, the next I was shielding my eyes to protect them from the merciless glare of the spotlight.

'This is the police,' a voice informed me, distorted by the megaphone. 'We have you completely surrounded.'

CHAPTER VIII

As a trap it was a complete fiasco, as bad as anything the Keystone Cops had managed to achieve on celluloid. If the police had waited quietly in the shadows until I'd reached the ground they could have seized me without any difficulty. Instead, the officer in charge had preferred to do things in style, doubtless thinking of the next day's press coverage, and had alerted me while I was still five stories up. There was even an open window beside me and I dived through it fast, intent on being out of sight before anyone started shooting. As I came out of my forward roll recovery across the carpet, a manœuvre which did absolutely nothing for my kidneys, the bedside lamp clicked on, revealing a balding, middle-aged man cosily tucked up in bed with a girl who couldn't have been a day over thirteen. When he saw my gun the man immediately ducked his head under the sheets, whinnying with fear, and the girl didn't seem to be particularly upset by my hurried departure from the room.

To my considerable relief the corridor was deserted, although a babble of noise from the surrounding rooms showed plenty of people had been woken up by the disturbance outside. Uncertain about my best move, I started down the stairs, realizing this was no permanent solution. Inevitably, at some time in the near future, I would bump into the police coming up and that would be that. On the other hand, hiding was equally out of the question for, if necessary, the police would tear the hotel apart to find me. Two flights down I abandoned the stairs, uncomfortably aware of the footsteps approaching from the other direction.

The long, green carpeted corridor I was running along was still unpopulated but this state of affairs wasn't likely to last and I was seriously considering whether the wisest course was to surrender when inspiration struck me, appropriately enough in the shape of a Roman Catholic priest. As I rounded the corner a bare five yards away from him he'd just unlocked the door to his room and he looked up in surprise at the wild apparition bearing down on him. My reactions were on the instinct level. One hand grabbed his collar, the gun went up under his nose and I bundled him inside the room, kicking the door closed behind us.

'I'm sorry, Father,' I panted, ready to clobber him if he tried to shout, 'but I need your clothes. Just do as I say and you won't be hurt.'

Enough liberal churchmen had been killed in Brazil over the past few months to dispel any doubts he might have had about clerical immunity and the priest accepted the situation philosophically, which was just as well. It was bad enough stealing his vestments without ruining all my hopes of redemption by laying violent hands on him. While he undressed I was busy tearing up a sheet which I used to bind and gag him once he was down to his underwear. All this he endured with almost stoical calm, even accepting the further indignity of being carried into the bathroom.

Acutely conscious of the growing hubbub outside I hastily pulled on the priest's robes over my own clothes. Examining myself in the mirror I had to admit the disguise couldn't have been bettered, even if black wasn't my colour. In particular I was thankful for the mores of a country which not only made sun-glasses a standard item of dress but could see nothing strange in wearing them on the darkest night. This was a custom I'd sneered at on many occasions in the past, now, endowed with new authority, I blessed the habit. The shades, combined with the hat, did a lot to conceal my battered features.

The corridors were filled with people when I left the sanctuary of the priest's room, most of them still in their night clothes, and there were the usual rumour mongers amongst them, their speculation ranging from revolution to multiple murder. Surrounded by an aura of holiness I remained aloof from useless conjecture, making my dignified way to safety. The first obstacle came in the person of the policeman stationed by the lifts. Assuming my most pious mien I simply behaved as though he wasn't there, pressing the button for the lift. The policeman approached me diffidently.

'Excuse me, Father,' he said apologetically. 'You'd better return to your room. There's a dangerous criminal loose in the hotel. A killer.'

Slowly I turned to face him, my head held low, knowing the encounter would be an acid test for my Portuguese. I spoke the language fluently but I didn't usually pretend I spoke it well enough to pass as a native Brazilian.

'There have always been killers in the world,' I intoned, feeling the sweat trickle down my back. 'They have never prevented the ministers of the church from doing their duty.'

This was a horrible, crappy line, one which would make me cringe with embarrassment when I thought of it in restrospect. Even Hollywood in the thirties could hardly have done worse. Fortunately the lift doors opened as I finished speaking and I swept majestically inside, not waiting to explain myself. Or to hear the policeman's comments on my accent. For two nerve-racking moments I stared gravely out of the open lift doors while the policeman gawped in, then the doors swished closed and the lift began to descend.

As I went down I was clammily aware that this had been the easy part, that the policeman could afford not to voice any objections because he knew there was another line of defence in the lobby. In fact there seemed to be dozens of policemen scattered around the place, many of them officers, and two men were guarding the revolving doors, machine pistols at the ready. Slowly I walked towards them, trying to convince myself I was a priest on an urgent errand of mercy, not a craven, quaking Englishman on the run from the police, his immortal soul in jeopardy for assaulting one of God's representatives on Earth. When I approached the door two machine pistols swung inwards to bar the exit.

'No one is to leave the hotel,' one of the policemen snarled unpleasantly.

His tone didn't display a glimmer of respect for the cloth and the bastard had all the hallmarks of a militant, died-in-the-wool atheist. Instinctively I performed the bravest act of my young life, gently pushing both guns out of my way, my hands leaving damp marks on the barrels.

'A man is dying,' I said solemnly. 'He needs me.'

If possible, this was a lousier line than the first and I went through the doors expecting either a command to halt or a bullet in the back. Neither eventuality occurred. Seconds later I was out in the street, pushing my way through the small crowd surrounding the entrance and past the police jeeps lining the kerb, their drivers leaning against the bumpers and only too glad they didn't have to chase dangerous, armed criminals inside the hotel.

As the real priest was likely to be discovered at any moment my natural inclination was to vanish over the horizon in a cloud of dust but, exercising iron restraint, I held myself down to a brisk walk until I reached the Kombi. Once there I abandoned all pretence.

Minus the clerical gear I drove flat out, staying ahead of the road blocks until I was forty miles from Caxias. Porto Alegre was surrounded by two distinct ethnic zones. The inner circle, including Novo Hamborgo and Sao Leopoldo, was predominantly German, so much so that until the war expectant mothers would board German ships in Porto Alegre harbour and have their babies beyond the three-mile limit to ensure German citizenship for their offspring. Inland, where the land rose, this merged into the wine-growing area and the more successfully integrated Italians took over. I was well up into the hills when, rounding a corner, I spotted the road block. There was nothing elaborate about it, just a red and yellow pole across the road and a jeep containing two policemen parked on the verge, but it wasn't something I could ignore.

Dutifully, I slowed down as the policemen stepped into the road, waiting until I was less than fifty yards away before I stamped on the accelerator. The Kombi's acceleration was nothing to write home about but what it lacked in speed it more than made up for in weight and it crashed through the flimsy barrier like a tank, sending the policemen diving for their lives. They were still sorting themselves out when I rounded the next bend, some three hundred yards away.

If I'd been travelling fast before, now I should have been driving for my life but my responses were becoming sluggish. Over the past day or two fear, anger and shock had been pumping bursts of adrenalin into my system at crucial junctures and I appeared to have exhausted the supply. The new threat left me absolutely cold and, hunched over the wheel, I was only aware of physical exhaustion, my eye sockets feeling as though they were coated with sandpaper. At the best of times I was no Stirling Moss and, under stress, I deteriorated to L-driver standard, clipping the verges at almost every corner. My poor driving, the narrow, winding road and the uncomfortably steep drops on one side or the other made disaster almost inevitable at the speed I was travelling, especially when they were combined with the tricky, half light of dawn. In fact I managed just five miles before it struck.

I was negotiating one of the rare downhill sections, uneasily ignoring the warning notices, when I failed to complete a left-hand bend which came back nastily at me, the narrow bridge only serving to complicate matters. Instead of following the road the Kombi hit the wooden railings of the bridge at an angle, ending up with the front wheels precariously balanced over a sheer drop to the fast-flowing river thirty feet below.

The one useful result of the collision was that I smacked my head painfully against the windscreen, waking myself up. My sense of urgency restored I hastily grabbed the money from the glove compartment, adding Melanie's peashooter as an afterthought. Luckily the police jeep must have been a slow starter because I could hear no sounds of pursuit as I clambered gingerly from the Kombi, praying it wouldn't slide into the river for a minute or two.

It was almost dawn and the birds were already breaking into joyous song at the approach of another day but I was in no mood to share their appreciation. Stationed at the rear of the Kombi I pushed with all my strength, nearly rupturing myself with the effort, and the vehicle didn't budge an inch. Changing tactics I tried lifting the back bumper and met with no more success. There was no time for anything else as police sirens were wailing in the distance, from both directions unless my ears deceived me.

Conceding defeat I stepped away from the Kombi and as I did so it tilted noiselessly forward of its own volition, then slid gently out of sight over the edge of the bridge. I didn't hang around to listen for the splash. The sirens were coming too close for comfort and I sprinted towards the cover of the woods at the far side of the bridge, not looking back until I was safely concealed amongst the trees.

The jeep I'd passed at the road block was first on the scene, having less than a minute in hand over the one which arrived from the opposite direction. Their advent proved there was something to be said for dangerous driving after all because if my incompetence hadn't caused me to smash into the bridge I would have been sandwiched between the two of them. The policemen were soon huddled round the gap in the railings and it wasn't difficult to guess what they were thinking. They expected me to be trapped inside the van, somewhere in the wreckage on the stream bed, and even when they failed to find my body they wouldn't be surprised. It was a hell of a drop from the bridge and the river had a strong current so they'd merely think my corpse had been swept downstream. Eventually someone would get to checking the woods but by then I'd be long gone.

I slept far longer than I'd intended and it was early evening before I breasted the brow of the low hill overlooking the de la Sagra fief. It had been a hard afternoon, my exertions leaving me hot, scratched and thirsty, so I sat on an outcrop of rock to smoke a Continental before facing the last quarter of a mile through the immaculately tended vines.

Ramon de la Sagra was a Spaniard, my friend and one of the greatest rogues in the world, almost too large for life. He maintained he was an anarchist, basing the claim on his family name, which I was certain he'd assumed, and his former membership of the Confederacion Nacional del Trabajo. He even had a tattered red and black flag over his mantelpiece, just to back up his story.

If he was to be believed, and I didn't, he'd been active in Barcelona during the Spanish Civil War and then fought with Buenaventura Durutti in Aragon and Madrid. Despite the impeccable record Bakunin or Kropotkin would have had considerable difficulty in recognising him as a disciple. Whatever his beliefs as a young man the years had turned Ramon into an old-time, feudal despot. The two hundred peasants on his vast estates acknowledged his laws, not those of Brazil, and his rule was so absolute it was a wonder he didn't establish Customs posts. The sole reason his serfs put up with him was that no one ever went hungry on the de la Sagra estates. For a man whose original capital had come from a Spanish bank robbery Ramon hadn't done at all badly.

The cigarette finished I trudged across the dry, crumbly soil between the vines, glad it was no more than a quarter of a mile. Ramon's dwelling place, an enormous, rambling bungalow, was in the centre of the village, the cottages of his employees grouped around it. Several of the villagers greeted me as I passed, some of them welcoming me by name, and the fact they knew who I was didn't worry me in the slightest. They would never divulge the information to an outsider unless their master instructed them to.

Ramon himself was seated on the verandah of his house, a stocky, bearded man with the inevitable bottle of wine in front of him. He existed in a permanent state of semi-inebriation, never completely sober and never incapably drunk. I was halfway across the clearing in front of his bungalow palace when he spotted me.

'Philis, my friend,' he roared, dark eyes twinkling with pleasure as he advanced on me, his friendly embrace powerful enough to crack a lesser man's ribs. 'What kept you so long? I was expecting you hours ago.'

'What?' I said weakly.

Weakness was an emotion I usually experienced when I was exposed to the full blast of Ramon's personality.

'Those pigs of policia said you'd been killed in the crash,' he explained. 'I knew they were lying.'

By this time I was sitting on the verandah with a glass of wine in my hand. Ramon's unexpected boom of laughter made me spill half of it.

'I would have loved to have seen that priest, trussed up like a turkey in his underwear,' he spluttered. 'You remind me of when I was young.'

'Heaven forbid,' I muttered uncharitably, dabbing at my sodden trousers. 'And for God's sake don't tell me I've got cojones.'

My remark passed unnoticed—there was no stopping Ramon once he'd started on one of his anecdotes.

'I shall never forget one village we took in the drive towards Saragossa,' he continued inexorably. 'The villagers were living on slops while the priest had a great storehouse packed to the rafters with food. We organized a feast for the whole village, with the priest serving at table, and before we shot him we made him set fire to his own church. It was a marvellous sight.'

'No wonder Franco won the war,' I commented acidly.

127

'Your mob did so much church burning and bank robbing there wasn't any time for fighting. Anyway, I'm not sure I believe you any more.'

'What do you mean?'

Ramon did his best to sound hurt.

'I've done some checking,' I told him. 'If you were with Durutti when he assassinated the Archbishop of Saragossa you were only nine years old.'

'It must have been some other bishop, then,' Ramon said off-handedly, suddenly eager to change the subject. 'Drink up your wine and we'll go in to see Rosita. She put on her best dress when I told her you were coming.'

Ramon had been a widower for the past twelve years so I'd never met his wife but it was easy to see Rosita must have inherited her good looks from her. Only eighteen, she was enough of a woman to make my adopted uncle role something of a chore and I would have liked to see her. Unfortunately, when I rose from the chair my legs went rubbery beneath me, my head started an unscheduled trip on a rollercoaster and the next thing I remembered was waking up in bed, my chest heavily bandaged, with the early morning sun shining through the unshuttered windows. I had the impression I must have been overdoing things.

All next day Rosita mollycoddled me unmercifully and I lapped it up, dozing in between meals and bandage changing, the total relaxation raising my morale one hundred per cent. When Ramon made his appearance before dinner I was ready for anything, including the two bottles of wine he'd brought with him. We'd seen them off and started on two more before I'd finished relating my misadventures.

'What do you intend to do now?' Ramon asked. 'You know you're welcome to stay here for as long as you like. Rosita would be only too glad of the company.'

I laughed at him, something the wine made easy.

'You know damn well I'm not staying here. You'd never speak to me again if I did. I want to get to Santos.'

'Good,' Ramon said, rising to his feet with a beam on

his face. 'I'll tell Rosita that we'll be leaving in the morning.'

This was a reaction I'd anticipated and I grabbed hold of Ramon's arm before he was out of range.

'You're not coming with me, Ramon,' I told him. 'I need your help with the transport but the rest I'll do alone.'

'Don't be ridiculous,' Ramon protested. 'Just because I'm getting old you think I'm incompetent as well. You're wrong.'

'It's not that at all,' I interrupted hastily, before he began regaling me with Civil War exploits. 'I'm only being realistic. Whatever happens I'm finished here in Brazil. Whether I catch up with Biddencourt and Gordinho or not I'll still have to leave the country. With you it's different. You've spent thirty years building up this place—it's your whole life. And you have Rosita to think about. You had your fight in Spain, this one is mine.'

Even a man as pigheaded as Ramon couldn't fail to appreciate that I was talking sense and he agreed that seeing me to Sao Paulo was as far as his direct involvement went. For a man in his position it was easy to arrange. All the year round lorries full of wine were plying between the Caxias area and Sao Paulo and, as one of the leading producers, a fair number of these lorries belonged to Ramon. In these circumstances it didn't involve much of a break with routine to lay on a special trip for me. Nevertheless, Ramon refused to be left out of the act entirely. Maintaining it was high time for one of his outings to Sao Paulo, when he turned the Praca Roosevelt on its ear, he took the wheel for the journey. Even so I was in Sao Paulo by nightfall the next day.

CHAPTER IX

THE SERVICES provided by Zephyr taxis had to rank
among the best in the world. Every fifteen minutes during
the day, and for most of the night, their comfortable,
roomy cars gave door-to-door portage between Sao Paulo
and Santos, cities forty-five miles apart, for the cruzeiro
equivalent of a few shillings. Price apart, the journey was
quite something and, seated in the front of the nine o'clock
taxi, I fully appreciated it. Sao Paulo, a megalopolis of
breathtaking architecture which erupted from the rich
terra rossa of the plateau, stood at a height of nearly
three thousand feet and in less than fifty miles the road
was down at sea level, with Santos as its terminus. It was
a clear morning, with no haze to spoil the spectacular
view, and three quarters of the way down from the plateau
Santos was already in sight. The beach could almost have
been an imitation Copacabana, a long, golden sweep of
sand flanked by its white hedge of skyscrapers, the rest of
the city stretching out behind until it was finally hemmed
in by the surrounding hills. On the far side of the city a
scattering of tall buildings made another break in the
general skyline, marking the commercial area around
the Praca Maua, and, close by, the ungainly bulk of the
cranes dominated the docks, still handling more coffee
than any other port in the world. All this was spread in
a panorama below me as the taxi spiralled down the last
few miles of the descent and approached the vast COSIPA
complex marking the entrance to the town. Although
I'd only been away for a few days it was like returning
home.

Of course, this brought its attendant difficulties. Brazilian cities were far more intimate than their British
counterparts and, despite the fact Santos was almost as
large as Leeds, there was no part of the city where I'd be

safe from recognition. News of my exploits in the south would have reached Santos ahead of me and word of my return would soon go round. I was going to need protection, powerful protection which would cost a lot of money. Quite possibly every cruzeiro I'd saved.

Until this was arranged there was no question of visiting either of my apartments and I had the taxi driver drop me on the front. Luckily Inspector Pinto was at police headquarters when I phoned him.

'It's Philis,' I said in response to his query.

'And to think I've been wearing a black armband,' Pinto lied shamelessly. 'Where are you calling from?'

'I have to see you,' I told him, ignoring the question. 'Alone.'

'Of course. You know I'm always at your service.'

'This is serious, Vicente. Can I trust you?'

'You have my word,' he said solemnly.

This completely reassured me. To my mind his word was worth about as much as a ninety-seven year old virgin.

'Meet me at the Atlantico in half an hour,' I instructed him. 'I'll be in the outside bar.'

As soon as he'd hung up I took a table in the garden of the Park Hotel which was directly across the street from the Atlantico, affording a good view of the proposed meeting place. Fifteen minutes later, as the first plain-clothes men began to infiltrate the area, I judged it expedient to leave the Park, ambling a few hundred yards along the front to one of the better sea food restaurants. There I reflectively munched my way through a large plate of camarao paulista, washing down the prawns with a couple of litres of chopp, before I contacted Pinto again.

'I'm ashamed of you, Vicente,' I told him once we were connected. 'After you'd given me your word as well.'

Pinto laughed happily.

'You're forgetting something, Philis. Now you're a criminal there's a price on your head.'

'Well, I don't know what the reward is but I can promise you I'm a damn sight more valuable on the hoof than I am in jail. That's what I want to talk to you about. Of course, if you prefer we can fix it up over the phone but ...'

I allowed my voice to tail off.

'No, no,' Pinto came in hastily. 'It would be far better if we met.'

'OK, I'll try the Atlantico again. Make sure you're alone this time.'

Repeating the stipulation was pure formality. Now I'd suggested paying him Pinto would come prepared to talk business, postponing thoughts of a second doublecross. Nevertheless he'd have plenty of support close to hand in case my offer wasn't up to par. It was my intention to ensure it was.

The Atlantico Hotel held a special position in Santos, two features, quite apart from the standard of service, making it stand out. Firstly, its situation couldn't be bettered, a mere street's breadth from the beach and bang on the busiest intersection in the city. Secondly, and far more important, there was its hundred yard long verandah bar, under cover but open on the street side, a bar which had a unique place in the mores of Santos society. Every night the lucky few packed the terrace, watching the colourful cavalcade going past while they ate and drank in comfort. The pavement in front of the bar was the arena for the traditional mating ritual of the city, the place where young women of marriageable age strolled past, hand in hand and sporting their most enticing plumage, and the youths strutted, endeavouring to exude machismo at every step. At noon, on a weekday, however, the bar was virtually deserted and I had a table to myself.

I'd been sitting there for ten minutes, more interested in bikini-clad passers-by than in my beer, when Pinto hove into sight, his drab, insignificant exterior concealing a drab, insignificant soul. We greeted each other without a great deal of enthusiasm. Pinto was wondering how he could collect whatever I had to offer and rake in the reward as well, I was thinking what a horrible little ponce he was, rather disgusted at having to deal with him.

'At the latest count you're wanted for murder, assault and resisting arrest,' Pinto said to start the ball rolling. 'I'm not sure I can do anything to help you.'

This was his subtle way of letting me know he was going to be expensive to buy. I grinned at him to show I understood.

'Mere technicalities,' I said airily. 'In any case, I'm dead. Or hadn't you heard?'

'You won't be dead for long—too many people in Santos know you. I shall have to arrest you in a day or two to prevent word getting back to my superiors.'

The preliminary fencing was beginning to bore me.

'I realize it's going to be difficult for you, Vicente. Three thousand US dollars should be more than enough to keep the patrolmen off my back. They're the only real threat.'

Pinto's eyes glazed over while he did a rapid conversion. It was a hell of a good bribe, probably the best he'd ever been offered, especially as he wasn't figuring on any of the money going further than his own pocket. There was no sense in sharing if he was going to have me arrested as soon as I'd handed over the dollars. Luckily I could read Pinto's venal mind like a book and knew he wasn't a man you could buy but could only secure his co-operation until something better came along.

'Of course,' I continued casually, sure I had him hooked, 'there's your cut to be considered as well. I'm prepared to give you, personally, another five thousand.' I paused to light a cigarette. 'I'll hand it over when my business in Santos is finished—a fortnight at the outside.'

'Two thousand five hundred now, the rest when you leave,' Pinto countered without hesitation, adapting superbly.

'Not a chance.'

After a moment's delay Pinto stuck out his hand.

'Let's shake on it,' he suggested.

He could afford to be friendly, thinking he'd made the deal of a lifetime. He wasn't to know five thousand dollars was my total cash reserve and two thousand of this was destined to see me out of the country. Pinto was going to turn nasty when he discovered he'd been conned, very nasty if I was a judge of character. This was something I'd have to bear in mind later.

The first step was to take a look at the *Arcadia* and, if possible, have a word with the captain. With this aim I took a taxi to the General Camera, the hub of the red light district and, until the advent of Reece, my centre of operations in Santos. Most people would probably have consulted the Port Authority to find out where the ship was anchored but I preferred to do things the easy way. As an essential part of business every bar in the zona had an up to date, accurate roster of all ships due, expected or present in the harbour. Many of the girls, with regulars on the various vessels, couldn't afford to get their dates mixed and the juggling I'd had to do in my line of work paled into insignificance beside what some of the tarts were involved in. The classic example was Dulcie, a lush octroon whose thing was marriage. Her score, unless she'd chalked up another while I was away, was two Englishmen, one German and, for God's sake, an Arab. She worked from the Bataan Bar and this was where I headed. For obvious reasons the schedule there was up to the second.

On second thoughts I decided it might have been wiser to consult the Port Authority after all. It took less than a minute to learn the *Arcadia* had docked at Pier 14 two days before and that the dockers weren't due to begin loading the coffee until the next day, extricating myself from the bar took well over an hour. News of my Reece-inspired arrest at the Stockholm had already passed into local legend, with garbled reports of my infamous exploits down south equally widespread. My arrival at the Bataan attracted acquaintances from every bar in the vicinity and I was deluged with questions, having to employ all the expertise of a lifetime's lying to keep them happy. In return I learned one invaluable fact. Someone, who was either Pepe or his double, had been ploughing up and down the street pumping people for information about me. I no longer had the slightest doubt about Joao's veracity.

A quick phone call to Paulista to arrange Pinto's first, and last, payment, then I set off to Pier 14 in the oppressive, afternoon heat. The *Arcadia* proved to be a smallish ship, badly in need of a few coats of paint. On board there was a sloppy looking Customs official, his olive uniform streaked with sweat. I raised a hand in greeting, took advantage of what shade there was in the lee of one of the sheds, undid my last but one shirt button and lit a cigarette.

I'd never been an avid observer of parked ships and I didn't bother to start cultivating the habit now. Instead I watched the man sitting in a DKW across the road who was going through the motions of reading a newspaper. For all I knew he really could be keeping abreast of world affairs. Perhaps he preferred being roasted alive to sitting under an electric fan with a cool drink, because with the temperature hovering around the 40 degrees Centigrade mark it must have been like trying to read in a blast furnace. Although he was a long way away and largely concealed by the newspaper it was impossible to miss his shirt, a Hawaiian affair tastefully decorated with blue, scarlet and yellow cowpats. On the count of bad taste alone he couldn't possibly be a friend. Whether he was an enemy or not I'd have to find out later.

Killing my cigarette I sweated off a couple of pounds walking the few yards to the gangplank, shared a dirty joke with the Customs man and went aboard. Up on deck it was still about as lively as the 'Marie Celeste' on a wet Monday and I didn't have enough energy to waste it hiking around looking for the watchman. Taking things easy, I climbed the steps to the bridge and flipped on the tannoy.

'Attention below decks, attention below decks,' I shouted. 'Torpedo off the port bow, iceberg dead ahead and kamikaze approaching from starboard. Don't panic but can anyone tell me how to find reverse?'

Thinking this over as I returned to deck level I decided the sun was killing my sense of humour. Apparently the crewman theoretically acting as watchman shared my opinion.

'Ha bloody ha,' he said in a distinct Liverpudlian accent before going to slash over the side.

He was a squat, hairy character with only the grubby towel round his waist between him and total frontal nudity.

'Are you the captain by any chance?' I enquired once he'd readjusted the towel. If he was the captain I was Little Lord Fauntleroy but it didn't cost anything to be polite.

'Do you think I'd be the only one aboard this floating craphouse if I was the captain?' he complained eloquently. 'Anderson won't be back until we're ready to up anchor. The condition he's likely to be in we'll be lucky to find the Atlantic, let alone hit England.'

I didn't take the remark all that seriously, especially as the watchman was exhibiting unmistakable symptoms of a massive hangover himself, his eyeballs so bloodshot they looked like crosses between Jaffa oranges and AA road maps. Feeling sociable I gave him a cigarette and leaned on the rail beside him. A breeze was blowing up to clear the air. In a couple of hours it might even register on the Beaufort scale.

'What do you want with Anderson?' the sailor asked.

'It's a business matter. Do you know where I can find him?'

The sailor shrugged his shoulders.

'He's in one of the bars down the road for sure but which one is anyone's guess. Have you met the old bugger before?'

'Never,' I admitted.

'Well, he shouldn't be too hard to recognise. When you see a wizened-up little sod sitting at a table by himself that'll be Anderson.'

This wasn't the most graphic of descriptions but I didn't press for further details—now I knew the captain's name was Anderson it would be easy to find him. When I left the ship the DKW was still in position and, on the spur of the moment, I crossed the road to have a closer look. Hawaii shirt casually glanced up as I passed and for a second we scrutinized one another at a range of a few feet, then we both turned our heads away, neither of us fooling the other. Fairish hair, blue eyes, pale skin, none of these were Brazilian characteristics, except in the German dominated south, towns like Curitiba or Joinville. Or Porto Alegre. The man could have been one of the Europeans working around the dockyard but I wasn't a great believer in coincidences. What with his appearance and his patent interest in the *Arcadia* it was easier to consider him as a yet unidentified member of the opposition.

Intuition wasn't sufficient cause to haul him from the DKW and trample him into the dust so I continued walking, hoping I hadn't been recognised. We hadn't met before, of this I was positive, and the chances were Hawaii shirt hadn't known me from Adam for although my photograph had figured prominently in the *Correio de Povo* down in PA it hadn't graced the reports in the nationals. On the other hand, if he had recognised me life should become really hectic. It could even turn into a race to see whether I found Gordinho and company first or they found me.

For the moment there wasn't much I could do except carry on working methodically and this involved locating Captain Anderson. It was all very well nurturing the idea of doing unpleasant things to Biddencourt and Gordinho but this was no simple task and I had absolutely no guarantee of success. On the credit side I'd already hurt their organization by destroying their laboratory and I was in a position to hit them even harder in Santos. Really I should have been able to achieve this without coming out into the open but I'd made a bad mistake. Before shooting Joao I should have made him tell me what name the cocaine was being exported under because I could hardly see Gordinho or Biddencourt putting their own names to the bills of lading. This was where Anderson should be able to help me.

By the time I'd hiked back to the General Camera I was hot, sweaty and footsore, with a persistent pain in my kidneys to remind me I should have been in bed, not trotting around in the sun. There were at last sixty bars Anderson could be patronizing and I'd no intention of doing the legwork myself when there was a vast reservoir of cheap labour at my disposal. Seventy-five per cent of the beggars in the zona were deadbeats pure and simple, characters straight from Brecht's 'Threepenny Opera'. A few minutes each day with a blunt razor blade and a dirty fingernail and I could have had my body covered with sores as revolting as theirs, and induced by the same method.

Serge, the man of my choice, was one of the minority and more deserving than most. There must have been a whole shipload of White Rusians who'd arrived in Santos after the war, people who'd fled to the Chinese treaty ports to escape from the Bolsheviks only to have Mao wished on them less than a generation later. Many of them had managed to pick up the threads again, others had been less fortunate, including two women working the strip who claimed they would have been princesses in a Tsarist Russia. Serge himself had arrived penniless, without his left arm and with no friends to help him. Whenever possible I put work his way, not out of pity but because I genuinely liked him. Finding Anderson for me was only a start to my present plans for him.

While Serge went to work I deposited myself in the

Night and Day, rather disappointed I had to listen to an Eva record instead of being entertained by the steel band. As things turned out this was no great loss, Serge reporting back before I'd finished my first drink.

'Anderson is at the Oslo,' he told me in English.

He was the only beggar I knew who could speak six different languages.

'Fine. Now that's sorted out how do you fancy following somebody for me? Do you think you can manage it without being spotted?'

'I can do it,' Serge answered soberly. 'I take it you want me to keep an eye on the captain.'

'Far from it. There's a character parked in a pale blue DKW down at Pier 14. The car has a Rio registration for what it's worth. The fellow inside looks German—thirtyish, fair complexion and hair, blue eyes and he's got a small scar over his top lip. As far as I could judge he's about my build but the best way to recognise him is by his shirt—it's blue, red and yellow, really bright so you should spot him a mile off assuming he's left the car. If he isn't where I last saw him scout around the Camera and see whether you can pick him up. I want to know everywhere he goes and, above all, everyone he meets. Got all that?'

'I've got it. Where do I contact you?'

'I'll give you my number,' I told him, scribbling down the phone number of my apartment on the Rua Maranhao. 'I'll be there some time tonight so keep phoning until you get through.'

'And what if I don't find him?'

'Don't let it worry you. Just do your best.'

Serge nodded and walked out of the bar as though I'd asked him to perform the most natural task in the world. Life had kicked him in the teeth so many times he'd lost the ability to be surprised and he hadn't even bothered to count the roll of money I'd handed him, just shoved it in his pocket. Although he'd been reduced to begging Serge had retained his dignity. This, together with his insistence on personal hygiene, was why he did so badly on his pitch.

I left more or less on Serge's heels, braving the sun for the couple of minutes it took me to reach the doubtful sanctuary of the Oslo. Like everywhere else the bar was pretty dead and it wasn't difficult to spot Anderson. As forecast he was alone, sitting in the back booth while he sneered at the other occupants of the bar, and it seemed I hadn't been given such a bad description after all. Looking at him antisocial was a word which sprang readily to mind and, to judge by the way his face was thrown together, he'd spent a lifetime sucking lemons. Before I discovered whether he had a disposition to match I picked up a cuba libre at the bar. Fortified by a quick pull at my drink I ambled over, hoping I was correct in my assumption that Anderson wasn't in Gordinho's pay.

'Do you mind if I join you for a minute?' I asked politely.

A pair of watery brown eyes focused on me.

'Bugger off,' he said hospitably. Although his voice was only slightly slurred he was a good three sheets to the wind. 'There are plenty of other seats.'

Obviously he wasn't overwhelmed with joy at bumping into a fellow countryman but, undeterred, I eased myself into the seat opposite him.

'I won't keep you long,' I said reassuringly.

'Too bloody true you won't,' Anderson said angrily, his hand moving to grip the neck of an empty cerveja bottle. 'I told you to clear off.'

Although he was going through the motions his belligerency lacked conviction and he was too far gone to be up to the effort. Either that or he still had sufficient hold on his faculties to appreciate I could break him in half if he did start anything. It was high time for a spot of the famous, patented Philis psychology.

'Have a drink,' I suggested.

This speech was a ticket to instant acceptance. Anderson

140

abandoned the beer bottle, slopped down the rest of his drink and shoved his glass across the stained, cigarette-scarred table top.

'Make it cognac,' he said. 'A large one.'

Immediately Anderson shot up a notch in my estimation because Brazilian cognac was real firewater, two or three times more potent than meths and the kind of drink which could send you blind in twenty minutes flat. Whenever I drank the muck I accompanied every tiny sip with a mouthful of iced water, operating on the certainty that if the cognac reached my stomach undiluted it was likely to carry straight on down until it burned its way through the soles of my feet. Anderson had just knocked back a good gill without coming up for air and he was not only still alive but game for more of the same medicine. Obviously he was no mere social drinker.

After I'd returned with his replenished glass we sat in sociable silence for a while. Anderson had reached critical mass, the drink I'd bought about to make or break him, and there was no sense in antagonizing him by rushing matters. My back was to the rest of the bar so it was a choice between looking at Anderson or at the mural behind him, neither alternative particularly stimulating, and I was glad when he finally acknowledged my presence.

'What do you want?' he asked suddenly. 'I've never seen you before.'

'That's right,' I agreed, not bothering to introduce myself. 'I want to know who ships coffee on the *Arcadia*.'

There was a certain lack of subtlety in the way I'd broached the subject but Anderson was so tanked up that finesse would have been wasted. He'd either give me the information I needed or tell me to bugger off again, in which case I'd have to buy him a few more drinks. In the event Anderson complied with my request, not raising any objections or displaying any inquisitiveness. All the six coffee exporters he mentioned were perfectly respectable, long-established businesses bar one.

'Lima and company is new to me,' I commented.

'You're lucky,' Anderson mumbled. After his brief re-surgence he was sinking fast.

'You've had trouble with them?'

'Not until this trip. We had a big nigger down at the ship yesterday morning, thinking he could throw his weight around because he was all tarted up in an expensive suit. The way he behaved you'd expect him to be shipping the crown jewels, not a few, lousy bags of coffee. I'm sur-prised he didn't ask me to move out of my cabin to make room for them.'

Anderson's voice dropped to a mutter and the few words I caught were distinctly uncomplimentary. As I only knew one Negro who had a similar effect on me I thought it worth while to go for the jackpot.

'Was his name Biddencourt by any chance?' I asked.

The only reply was a disinterested shrug so I tried a different tack.

'Did you notice whether he had a ring on his right hand with a ruddy great green stone set in it?'

'That's right,' Anderson answered slowly, flashing me a malevolent glance. 'Is he a friend of yours?'

'Not exactly,' I hastened to explain, 'but he's the man I'm looking for. Do you know where I can find him?'

'Under a bloody stone most likely.'

Although Biddencourt appeared to have made quite an impression there was nothing more Anderson could tell me. Knowing what I did it was easy to guess why Bidden-court had been so particular about the storage of the coffee—with God knew how many thousands of pounds worth of cocaine concealed in the coffee bags he'd want to ensure they were in safe hands. Anderson wasn't to appreciate this, of course, and I'd no intention of en-lightening him. After all, it was in my interests for the contraband to reach Liverpool safely.

It wasn't until I'd finished my phone call to Ramon in Sao Paulo that I spotted Hawaii shirt. The full title of Gordinho's front organization was Lima Filhos e Cia.,

SA, I'd checked in the directory, and this snippet of information was all I needed to round off the telegram to Liverpool Ramon was going to send for me. I could have dispatched it from Santos but I felt safer having the message sent from Sao Paulo. No one was likely to intercept it there and, whatever else happened, the cocaine wouldn't get through to the distributors in England. As a start to my vendetta this wasn't at all bad and I turned away from the telephone filled with a kind of awe. Not everyone was as intimately associated with a genius as I was.

This was when I saw Hawaii shirt, an occurrence which peeled away a couple of layers of my complacency. He was sitting near the front of the bar, conscientiously ignoring me and engaged in animated conversation with the Ugly Sisters. It was well within the realms of possibility that he'd finished reading his newspaper, had purely by chance picked on the Oslo in preference to fifty other bars and, desirous of feminine company, had lost his heart to a pair of dikes who looked as though they made their living by wrestling in mud. For a full tenth of a second I wholeheartedly embraced this theory, then natural cynicism took over. Philis was being followed and, to put it mildly, Philis wasn't at all pleased. This meant I'd almost certainly been recognised, a complication I could have done without.

Evidently Hawaii shirt hadn't read his rule book properly because he stopped ignoring me when I made for the exit, moving from his table to block my way. I didn't break stride and he was on the retreat as he spoke.

'You're Philis, aren't you?' he said.

I nodded in acknowledgement and screeched to a halt, taken aback not so much by what he'd said as by the way he'd said it. Hawaiian shirt had not only sounded friendly, he'd addressed me in perfect, unaccented English, the kind which usually indicates an expensive education at a good public school.

'My name is Peter Collins,' Collins continued.

'Congratulations,' I told him, allowing him to usher me to the table where the Ugly Sisters were waiting.

For some reason Collins was embarrassed, uncertain how to begin, and I had no intention of bailing him out. If he had a guilty conscience he deserved it.

'I'm glad you're not dead,' he began awkwardly, 'but . . .'

'So am I,' I interrupted quickly, 'and there's a point I'd like to make before you start on the apologies. The women who work around the docks pick up the most unlikely languages, including English.'

Marlene, the dominating figure in the lesbian couple, simpered at me across the table and made a rude gesture while Collins blushed. He was about as comfortable in the Santos zona as I would have been at a Buckingham Palace garden party and I took pity on him, tossing a banknote to Marlene.

'Why don't you two girls go somewhere and have fun together,' I suggested.

'You know, Philis,' Marlene said before she left, affectionately twisting my ear, 'every time I see you I realize why I hate men.'

I knew she didn't mean this but, just the same, I was glad when she didn't take my ear with her.

'What happened to Reece?' Collins asked.

'I don't know exactly but he's dead.'

'What a mess.'

Collins gave a grimace of disgust, a sentiment I wholeheartedly agreed with, then offered me a cigarette. I accepted it, and the light to follow, leaving Collins to bear the burden of the conversation.

'I've a boss called Pawson,' he informed me. 'He told me to proffer his apologies for the clumsy way you were dragged into this business. Whether you accept the apology or not is up to you.'

'Pawson expected me to be alive then?'

'He wasn't sure but he had a feeling you might be. That car accident at the bridge seemed too good to be true. Now

144

I know for certain I'm authorized to offer you full-time employment with our department. Because of us you'll have to leave Brazil so you'll need a job to go to.'

Although I wasn't particularly amused I laughed in Collins's face, wondering whether there was any limit to this fellow Pawson's nerve.

'Listen, friend,' I said. 'I'll give you just two reasons why I don't want anything to do with your precious chief —Lydia Pirelli and Otto Schmidt. If that isn't enough I can give you a quick run down of some of the minor changes in my own life since he started playing God.'

Collins sighed and passed a hand across his face. He looked tired but he was getting no sympathy from me.

'I can appreciate your attitude,' he conceded. 'Just the same I think you ought to take time to consider the proposition. From where you're sitting the department has made an unjustifiable intrusion into your private life but it was the most efficient way of breaking up Biddencourt's operation, even if several people were hurt in the process. You flushed Biddencourt out into the open and we got as far as the *Arcadia* from the British end. Now there's just the final mopping up to be done.'

'Terrific,' I commented, rising to my feet. 'Absolutely top hole. You get on with your mopping up but let me give you a word of advice. Stay well clear of me or I might be tempted to make an unjustifiable intrusion into your private life.'

When I left the Oslo Collins was still sitting at his table, looking more tired than ever.

Despite the warning I knew Collins had no intention of losing me. Apparently we'd reached the *Arcadia* from opposite directions, myself after a long, hard slog which had taken me to Porto Alegre, Rio Grande and a farmhouse outside Pelotas, Collins as a result of investigations in Britain. Unless he was an idiot, which seemed extremely unlikely, Collins must have realized that my interest in the ship could only indicate an equal interest in Biddencourt and, judging by the way he'd offered me a job, he thought I stood a good chance of unearthing him. This assumption was indubitably correct but I'd no desire to give him a helping hand—I preferred to work alone rather than with someone who was inspired by motives different from my own. Under other circumstances I might have grown to like Collins; if he tried to keep tabs on my movements, as he probably would, he would be nothing more than an embarrassment.

Exactly what I did to combat the new situation depended on how successful Serge had been. If he'd been on the ball and was already tailing Collins it would make things simpler for me, even though I'd have a small procession behind me. All I'd have to do in this case would be to lose Collins and leave it to Serge to trail him to base. On the other hand, if Serge hadn't made contact, life would become much more complicated. Losing Collins would be no more of a problem but I hated to think of him mooching around Santos without my knowing what he was up to.

To my relief Serge was leaning against a wall twenty yards down the road when I exited from the Oslo, blending in nicely with the scenery. I gave him a big wink before I turned into the Zanzibar next door where, as I'd hoped, Rosa was sitting, chatting with three sailors. She scowled ferociously in reply to my smile but ditched her customers in double time and came over to join me at the bar. Tall, a good five foot ten with a Junoesque body to match, Rosa was the best-looking Negress I'd seen, bar none, and she had a brain as well. Considering what she had to offer she was wasted on the clientele.

'This is an unexpected honour,' she said, once I'd set up the drinks. 'It's not often you're able to spare me a few minutes of your valuable time.'

'You make me feel such a louse,' I answered, fighting back the tears. 'You know you're the only woman in my life.'

Rosa laughed.

'Along with two hundred others you mean. What is it this time?'

'Nothing much. I just want you to play truant for half an hour or so.'

'Don't tell me you've turned into a short-time merchant,' she said with a grin, her eyebrows raised. 'I finish here at seven.'

'I can't wait that long,' I told her, grabbing her thigh in mock passion. 'You know how you affect me.'

'I'm not surprised you feel like a louse,' Rosa responded, not at all put out by my mick taking. 'One of these days you'll get a hell of a shock when I present you with the bill. Wait a minute and I'll fix things with Max.'

In less than five minutes she was back, carrying a handbag the size of a small holdall. When I put an arm round her waist she raised her eyebrows again but didn't comment until we were outside in the street.

'Where to now, O master?' she asked.

'The nearest short-time hotel,' I told her. 'Where else?'

The hotels in the Santos dock area weren't the kind which would find a place in Baedeker or the AA guide and copulation centres would be an apt description of their function. From the outside they were ugly, inside they were sordid, the rooms unvaryingly uniform in their layout—a double bed adorned with soiled linen, a couple of chairs for clothes, hand towels for post coital ablutions and a broken-down dressing table. Rosa protested every step of the way to the room I'd booked, reminding me we both had clean, comfortable apartments. When we arrived she finally rebelled, her nose wrinkled in disgust.

'I don't know what you're up to, Philis,' she said, on the point of leaving, 'but I'm certainly not staying here.'

I hauled her back before she had a chance to move far and locked the door.

'Don't get yourself in a lather,' I said equably. 'Much as I fancy you this décor does have a definite passion-

147

killing effect. I'm afraid you do have to stay here, though. Just for fifteen minutes or so.'

Rosa eyed me suspiciously.

'What will you be doing? Taking dirty photographs?'

'Not exactly,' I told her. 'I'll be slipping through the back door. I've a shadow I want to lose.'

Immediately Rosa became serious, all traces of flippancy gone as she looked at me with concern.

'Is it serious?' she asked anxiously.

'You could say that,' I admitted, exaggerating for her benefit.

She came into my arms and bussed me enthusiastically.

'Be careful, Philis.'

'Don't worry,' I assured her, gently disengaging myself. 'I always am.'

In the early days in Santos, when I'd been establishing myself, there had been several occasions I'd found it expedient to do a vanishing act and the hotel had been selected with some care. Collins, however, lived up to my expectations. As I left the garbage-filled back yard, emerging in a narrow side street, I glanced up towards the General Camera. There wasn't much to see, just a pale blue DKW parked on the corner. Behind the wheel, staring down the side street, was a man in a brightly decorated Hawaii shirt. Collins had chosen to ignore my warning.

CHAPTER X

'WHERE TO?' the taxi driver asked.

'Into town,' I instructed him. 'And drive slowly.'

Carlos flashed me a conspiratorial smile before he returned his eyes to the road. The DKW had started off behind us and I wanted to give Serge a chance to take a taxi of his own. The slow pace would also allow me time to plan my next move.

'You're not going to the big match?'

With this question Carlos suddenly became the recipient of my full attention.

'The thought had occurred to me,' I lied. 'Who is it they're playing?'

'Corinthians.' A note of contempt in his voice reproved my ignorance of such an important fact. 'It should be a good game.'

The nod with which I acknowledged this remark was halfhearted in the extreme. Santos possessed the best football team in Brazil, one of the top half dozen club teams in the world, so most matches they played were good. With several of the national team, including the incomparable Pele, they had a lot going for them but this was one occasion when the football angle didn't interest me overmuch. I was far more intrigued by the thought of thirty thousand spectators packed into the cramped municipal stadium.

'What time is the kick-off?' I asked.

'Seven o'clock. There's plenty of time to get there if you want to go.'

'I do want to,' I told Carlos. 'Very much.'

It was ludicrously easy. Carlos dropped me bang outside one of the entrances and, while Collins tried to find a parking space for his car, I flashed my season ticket and trotted briskly up the concrete steps to the terraces. The kick-off was less than ten minutes away, the curtain raising reserve match already finished, and the ground was filled to capacity. At the head of the steps a burst of cheering greeted the loudspeaker announcement that Pele was definitely playing but, as my plans didn't include watching the match, I didn't add my voice to the general jubilation. Instead I determinedly began pushing my way through the crowd, aiming to be close to one of the other exits when Collins put in an appearance.

Fifteen yards into the crowd I stopped pushing, undergoing a rapid change of heart. Six rows down and ten

149

yards in front of me I'd caught a glimpse of a face I recognized, the unmistakable profile of Joao's Indian friend, Pepe. For a fraction of a second the hairs at the back of my neck bristled as I smelled a trap, then I recalled that half an hour previously I myself hadn't known I'd be coming to the stadium. This was one occasion I had to believe in coincidences and it was a coincidence I liked. With Pepe under surveillance Gordinho and Biddencourt were as good as in the bag.

All things considered I quite enjoyed the football, despite the unobtrusive eye I had to keep on Pepe. Ten minutes from the final whistle the scores were level and there were only two people in the stadium not totally absorbed in the play, the other being Collins who was a couple of rows behind me. It was high time I lost him.

Unhurriedly I made for the aisle, certain he'd follow me, and I waited for him at the head of the stairs. Collins stopped when he saw me, staying well out of range of a fist or foot.

'You're not waiting for the finish then,' he grinned, sensing I was going to try to take him and confident he could deal with me.

'I was getting nervous with you breathing down my neck,' I explained. 'Anyway, I've pressing business.'

The foul smelling toilets were half-way down the stairway, completely deserted at this crucial juncture in the game, and the footsteps behind me faltered uncertainly as I went in, Collins wondering what I was up to apart from the obvious. He suspected I wanted him to follow me in so that I could jump him but against this he had to balance the possibility of me slipping out through a window. He was still dithering outside the door when I emerged half a minute later, casually adjusting my dress.

'Don't look so worried,' I told him. 'I'm not going to get rid of you just yet. First I want a ride in your car.'

I'd always been told that lying was wrong but I was only being kind, allowing Collins a second's relaxation before the stiffened fingers of my left hand caught him in the diaphragm region. He went back against the wall, all the steam taken out of him, and I bent my gun round his ear to put him out of his misery. Grabbing him under the armpits I dragged his unconscious body into one of the cubicles, locked it from the inside and left by clambering over the door. With me I took the contents of his pockets, including the keys to the DKW.

Serge was lounging around outside the stadium and he was surprised when I walked up to him, looking over my shoulder as if he expected to see Collins behind me.

'What's happened?' he asked.

'Our friend has a bad headache,' I explained. 'He's decided to rest for a while. He should put in an appearance in about fifteen minutes. When he does, carry on as before, I still want to know everything he gets up to. To make things a bit easier for you I'm going to borrow his car. If I can find where he parked it, that is.'

'It's over here,' Serge said, turning to lead the way.

On the spot I decided to double the amount of money I'd intended to pay Serge for his assistance. Not because he knew where the DKW was parked, this was only to be expected, but because of the stoical calm with which he greeted every new turn of events. He was exhibiting the most remarkable lack of curiosity I'd ever come across.

Sticking to form, Serge watched me appropriate the car without a flicker of expression. Once the engine was ticking over I rolled down the window and stuck out my head.

'Don't forget to ring in later tonight,' I told him. 'Try me at midnight. If I don't answer then phone in every half hour until I do.'

The Russian nodded phlegmatically and I drove the DKW the two hundred yards back to the stadium, hoping Pepe wasn't one of the early birds who were already straggling away. The longer I had to wait the more I worried but my concern died a natural death when Pepe appeared in one of the last dribbles of spectators to leave the ground. If he'd opted to walk wherever he was going

I would have had to abandon the car, as it was he lived up to my expectations by preferring to take a taxi. At the prices cab fares were no one with money in his pocket was likely to walk farther than a quarter of a mile.

Pepe had no reason to suspect he was being followed and, to guarantee his continued ignorance, I stayed a discreet distance behind the taxi as it cut through the residential back streets. Considering my streak of good fortune since returning to Santos it was a bit much to expect to be led directly to Gordinho's headquarters, too much in fact. When he reached the junction with the Ana Costa, where the taxi turned left towards the beach, I allowed three cars to slip between the DKW and the taxi but the precaution was wasted because Pepe's destination, one of the city's better pizzarias, was less than three hundred yards distant. I drove past, parked and settled down to wait him out, doing my best to ignore the anguished distress signals from my own stomach. A square meal would have done something to sop up the excess alcohol I was shipping inside.

Shortly before ten Pepe reappeared, not bothering with a taxi this time as his new objective was a cinema three minutes' walk down the street. The film showing was *Direito de Nascer*, an ancient, sloppy tear jerker which made Coronation Street seem like a pure art form, and I wasn't tempted to follow him in. Nor did I fancy remaining cooped up in the car for a couple of hours. So far Pepe had displayed every indication of being engaged in the aimless pursuit of pleasure and, with the show not finishing until midnight, I didn't think it likely he'd be seeing anyone I was interested in before morning. He'd had his quota of football, followed up with a good meal and was now goggling at the wonders of the silver screen. Putting myself in his shoes, it was a fair bet he wouldn't object to rounding off the night with an enjoyable, health giving screw and I'd always fancied myself as a ponce. With this in mind I moved the car from the Ana Costa, where it was a trifle too conspicuous for my liking, then phoned through to Max at the Zanzibar.

'Philis here,' I said to break the glad tidings. 'I'm going to ask you to do me a favour.'

'You surprise me,' Max answered, displaying undue cynicism. 'That's all you ever do, ask for bloody favours. What is it this time?'

'Relax, it isn't going to cost you a cruzeiro. All you have to do is send someone round to Rosa's place. Tell her I'd like to speak to her.'

'She'll be with a customer at this hour,' Max protested.

'You're probably right. Tell her it's urgent, a matter of life and death. She'll come.'

Max mentioned something about me having a bloody nerve but he did send someone off. There was time to finish one cigarette and start on another before Rosa picked up the phone, sounding out of breath. If she'd been with a customer she didn't mention it.

'Has anyone ever told you you're a bastard, Philis?' were her exact words.

'Now you mention it I do remember the odd occasion,' I admitted, 'but it was only in fun.'

'I bet. You'd better make your story good.'

'It's one of my best, far too good to waste over the telephone. Doll yourself up in your Sunday best, hop into a taxi and I'll tell all. I'm on the Ana Costa in a bar opposite the Carioca cinema.'

'You're sure it's important?'

'Vitally,' I assured her.

'OK,' Rosa said, still sounding doubtful. 'When you say Sunday best what do you mean?'

'Exactly what I said. To give you a hint of the goodies to come I can tell you there's a man I want you to solicit for me.'

'That should make a lovely change,' she said drily. 'I'll see you in half an hour.'

On this slightly bitter note she hung up. All the same there was one very nice thing about the line of business I'd been involved in for the past few years. I might spend my life associating with tarts and criminals but their friendship was worth a hell of a sight more than the kind to be found in the upper echelons of society.

Rosa showed up in a sexy, little white mini-dress which did absolutely nothing to conceal the fact that she was the biggest and the best in town. Her faith in me still wasn't unquestioning and, as there was an hour before Pepe should be leaving the cinema, I turned the famous Philis charm up to full blast, determined to allay her misgivings. To achieve this I explained partially, and not wholly truthfully, what had happened in Rio Grande do Sul, concentrating chiefly on Lydia. Maudlin sentimentality was something I'd exploited before and the quickest way of removing Rosa's doubts so the lies were more than an intellectual exercise. When I finished Rosa had tears in her eyes and I only hoped I hadn't laid it on too thick —everything would be ruined if she took a knife to Pepe herself.

'Just tell me what I have to do,' she said, her voice husky.

I squeezed her hand appreciatively, marvelling at the depths I could sink to when I really put my mind to it. Playing on the sentiments of someone who was more than half in love with me herself by telling her about my relationship with another woman was a form of emotional blackmail even I had never resorted to before.

'Thanks, Rosa,' I said quietly. 'The man I'm interested in is at the Carioca. I'll point him out to you when he leaves. Do you think you'll be able to hook him?'

'It's my job, isn't it?' she replied, showing I'd inspired a touch of self-pity. 'What do I do with him once he's in tow?'

'You take him to my apartment on the Rua Maranhao. Here's the key.'

'He might want to go somewhere else,' Rosa pointed out, accepting the key.

'In that case use your powers of persuasion, though I

can't see you having much difficulty on that score. If he's interested enough to be picked up he's not likely to quibble over whether he plays at home or away.'

'I wouldn't be too sure,' Rosa persisted. 'Some men are funny that way.'

'Go with him anyway,' I decided. 'You'll just have to find some way of letting me know where you are.'

Rosa nodded her agreement and belted back a man-size shot of whisky. It was scotch, not the Brazilian rubbish, but her palate didn't seem to be up to appreciating it.

'What are you going to do when I've delivered him?' she asked curiously.

'I was thinking along the lines of a quiet man to man chat.'

'It should be worth watching,' she said, pushing forward her glass. 'I might sit in.'

Despite Rosa's confidence I wasn't sure the scheme was one of my better ideas. She was the type of woman any normal hetero male would want to drag on to the nearest bed but, off-hand, I could think of about seven hundred and thirty-five reasons why Pepe might not be agreeable to falling in with my plans. Like a double rupture, for example.

The permutations of what might go wrong were so endless Rosa's success in one minute flat gave me as big a lift as winning the national lottery would have done. Personally, I thought her technique was dead corny, although whatever it lacked in sophistication it certainly made up for in effectiveness. Pepe came out of the cinema with the rest of the audience, making things easy by stepping to the kerb in order to flag down a taxi, I pointed him out and Rosa steamed off across the road. She reached the far pavement no more than a yard from Pepe and when she dropped her handbag it virtually landed on his foot. She'd been holding the clasp open so all the bric-à-brac inside spilled on the ground and Rosa bent down to retrieve it. Within seconds every red blooded male in the vicinity had been attracted to the scene, the mass movement close to qualifying as a stampede, with Pepe bang in the centre of the scrum. The dress Rosa was wearing could hardly be described as modest at the best of times, with her squatting on the pavement it must have concealed all of a square centimetre round her navel.

When the mêlée eventually sorted itself out Rosa and Pepe came up together. For a second they stayed at the kerb chatting, then Pepe took her arm and they walked off. Although he was walking away from me he was leering so much he had a crease in the back of his neck.

I didn't wait to see whether steam started to come out of his ears, wanting to be back at the apartment to catch Serge's twelve-thirty phone call. In the event I had ten minutes to spare.

'Make it snappy, Serge,' I said when the call came through. 'I'm expecting company.'

'That's easy,' Serge answered, 'because there isn't much to tell. He left the stadium about ten minutes after everyone else, looking as though he still had a headache, and he didn't seem particularly surprised to find the car gone. He only spent a couple of minutes searching for it, then he began walking. All the way back to Indaia Hotel. He's been there ever since. If he's got any sense he'll be in bed.'

'All right, I can take a hint. Just make sure you're back at the hotel bright and early in the morning.'

'Sure. I'll phone you then.'

With this out of the way I settled down in the darkened apartment to await the arrival of Rosa and Pepe. I also wondered whether I'd made the right decision in coming to the Rua Maranhao. Reece had learned about my bolt-hole there and would undoubtedly have passed the information on. On the other hand, Collins would be aware that I knew he knew about the apartment and should also have guessed I was intent on avoiding him. This being the case he should expect me to be hiding somewhere else. I hoped my assumption was correct or, alternatively, that Manuel gave me plenty of warning if I was wrong.

I'd instructed Rosa to stop off for a drink on her way to the apartment, to make sure I had time to take Serge's call, but she and Pepe must have had a bottle apiece because it was nearly two in the morning when I heard the lift ascending, its laboured creaking a testimony to Brazilian engineering efficiency.

They made a lovely couple, Pepe's hand resting familiarly on Rosa's buttock as they came in, about as high as he could reach considering Rosa topped him by a good six inches in her high heels. It was almost a kindness to clamp my left arm across his throat and jam the barrel of my gun up his right nostril. If the randy little Indian had tried what he was thinking of Rosa would probably have broken his back.

'If you're thinking of shouting forget it,' I said, my Lon Chaney accent not quite coming off in Portuguese. 'I don't want blood on the carpet.'

Pepe guessed it was his blood I was talking about and didn't make a sound. My forearm was pressing so hard against his Adam's apple he couldn't have done so anyway and one glance at my face over his shoulder was all the extra incentive he needed. Perhaps he remembered what he'd helped to do to me in that farmhouse kitchen.

'I'm going to release you now,' I told him, 'but don't get any silly ideas.'

Releasing my grip on his neck I pushed him away. In all the westerns I'd seen the Indians had remained impassive whatever the circumstances but apparently this didn't hold good for Brazilian Indians because Pepe was giving a superb imitation of being scared stiff. Rosa, on the other hand, had parked herself in an armchair and was casting longing glances at the well stocked cocktail cabinet.

'What do you want with me?' Pepe asked, his voice so unsteady it must have ranged through three octaves.

Although this was understandable under the circumstances it was still a damn stupid question. I suppose I could have played along, thrown out a few blood-curdling threats for effect, but I couldn't be bothered.

'Leave the questions to me,' I said curtly. 'Just take off your clothes.'

'Take my clothes off?' Pepe echoed, his voice control not improving at all.

Rosa sniggered rather unkindly from her armchair.

'That's right,' I said patiently. 'And make it snappy. It's late and I want to get to bed.'

Until I waggled my gun under his nose Pepe had a lot of other questions on the tip of his tongue but the threat had him removing his clothes with an alacrity which would have put a professional strip-tease artiste to shame. Not that anyone would have paid to see what he had to offer and, if there'd been any sand handy, I'd have probably kicked it in his face.

'You're offending the lady,' I told him, once he was stripped to the buff. 'Lie down on your face with your hands behind your back.'

He obeyed without hesitation, a gratifying reaction. It seemed he might forget the mock heroics, an attitude which should save us both a great deal of trouble.

'Rosa,' I continued. 'I left a length of clothes line in the kitchen. Be a love and fetch it for me.'

She smiled happily to show how much she was enjoying the performance and wandered off to do as I'd asked. When she returned I gave her the gun, making her hold it close to Pepe's head while I practised a few Boy Scouts' knots on him. Not that he seemed disposed to make a fuss. The spreading damp patch beneath him was ruining my carpet but it did show he was in the right frame of mind to answer a few polite questions. None too gently I used my foot to turn him over on his back.

'It wasn't my fault,' he started gabbling once his face was out of the carpet. 'It was all Biddencourt's doing. I didn't want to hurt . . .'

'Shut up,' I ordered, silencing him with a quick boot in the ribs. 'From now on you only speak when you're spoken to. Understood.'

Pepe was so effusive in his compliance I almost risked damaging my foot some more. Instead I turned to Rosa.

'Thanks a lot for your help, Rosa, but I don't think there's any need for you to stay now. It may not be very pretty to watch. Use the phone to call a taxi.'

Rosa shook her head decisively.

'You're not going to kick me out at this hour in the morning. I'll stay here.'

After all she'd done for me it would have been churlish to argue with her.

'In that case grab yourself a drink and use the spare bedroom,' I told her. 'I'll try not to make too much noise.'

Rosa came over, affectionately draped her arms around my neck and treated me to one of her slow burn kisses.

'Exactly why do you think I've been trotting around all day obeying your slightest command?' she asked when we surfaced for air.

'You're a slave to my irresistible charm,' I suggested modestly.

'You're so right,' Rosa agreed. 'That's why I shan't be using the spare room.' She kissed me again. 'Don't be long. I'll be waiting for you.'

Once he'd finished emptying his bladder over the carpet I dumped Pepe on the sofa and he sprawled across it twitching uncontrollably, almost as if his entire nervous system had broken down. Surprisingly the spectacle didn't provide me with any particular satisfaction, indeed his pathetic defencelessness even inspired a momentary twinge of pity. Two or three days before, given the same circumstances, I'd probably have worked him over with a baseball bat, now I lit two cigarettes and stuck one of them between Pepe's lips. He needed the nicotine badly, the way the smoke came through his nostrils in small puffs instead of a continuous stream bearing testimony to his nervousness. I straddled a chair and looked at him over the back, my chin resting on my forearms.

'I've had a long, hard day, Pepe, and I want to get to

bed.' My voice was controlled and reasonable. 'I definitely don't want to waste a lot of time messing around with you.'

At this Pepe gulped so hard he nearly swallowed his larynx, the cigarette falling from his mouth. I retrieved it from the sofa and stubbed it out in an ashtray.

'The way I see the situation I've two alternatives,' I went on. 'I can take a leaf from your book and use persuasion to make you talk, just stick a piece of plaster over your mouth and keep on hurting you until I decide you're ready. That's the first alternative.'

Before I threw in the part which I hoped was going to save me a great deal of strenuous, unpleasant work I gave Pepe an opportunity to mull over the things I might do to him. If his complexion had deteriorated any further he would have been well on the way to becoming the world's first grey Indian.

'The other alternative strikes me as being far more satisfactory for both of us,' I continued, judging he'd had long enough to elaborate his nightmares. 'To put it in a nutshell, you co-operate voluntarily and I guarantee to let you go. Think the proposition over.'

Leaving him to his thoughts I went through to the kitchen to brew myself a cup of coffee, no doubts clouding my mind as to what his decision would be. When I returned Pepe was looking a lot healthier, although he still seemed capable of crapping himself at the drop of a hat.

'How do I know I can trust you?' he asked shakily, before I could seat myself.

There was no satisfactory answer to this, and he knew it, but he was so tensed up he had to ask.

'Apart from my word of honour as an English gentleman, which isn't worth a damn to anyone, there's no absolute guarantee I can give. To be quite frank, I don't care a hoot whether I have to kill you or not. You're of no importance at all, just a hired, mindless sadist. I do mind about your bosses, though, and if you help me to get them I'll be grateful, so grateful I shan't bother to kill you. Play this the hard way and you have my solemn promise that you're a dead man as soon as I've extracted the information I'm after.'

There was only one thing Pepe could say and he said it.

'I'll co-operate,' he told me, after only the slightest hesitation.

His faith in my word wasn't great but, from his point of view, he was on to a hiding to nothing. Like Joao before him, his relish for torture was restricted to the aggressor's role.

'That's easy to say,' I pointed out. 'Just remember one thing. Try anything clever, anything at all, and our bargain is off.'

Pepe licked his lips nervously.

'I'll tell the truth,' he promised. 'I swear it.'

'You'd better,' I said grimly, although I believed him implicitly. He would have betrayed his own mother to save his skin. 'For a start you can tell me where to find Biddencourt and Gordinho.'

'They're staying at different hotels,' Pepe replied hastily, desperately eager to convince me of his good faith. 'Gordinho is at the Hotel Santos and Biddencourt is staying at the Inglaterra.'

'That sounds reasonable. How many men have they got with them in Santos?'

'There's only me. They didn't anticipate any trouble.'

'Only you?'

Pepe nodded so I threw the half full cup of black coffee into his lap, regardless of what it would do to my sofa. The coffee had cooled sufficiently not to scald Pepe but it was hot enough to make him shriek with pain. Of a sudden he was twitching again.

'What did you do that for?' he protested shrilly, looking as though he might burst into tears. 'It's the truth.'

'Like hell it is. What about the cover business, Lima Filhos? You're not going to convince me that's a ghost outfit.'

'You've got it wrong,' Pepe pleaded. 'As far as the staff

there is concerned they think it's a legitimate coffee firm. They don't know anything about the cocaine.'

Belatedly I regretted wasting the coffee. I was feeling thirsty and I suspected Pepe was telling me the truth.

'All right,' I conceded. 'When will Biddencourt and Gordinho be expecting to see you again?'

'Not until tomorrow night,' Pepe answered, patently relieved by the change of subject. 'We're all meeting together at ten.'

'You've no duties during the day then?'

'Not tomorrow. Biddencourt has to go to Lima Filhos to plant the cocaine in the coffee and Gordinho has business of his own. The only reason I'm seeing them at all is because they're closing shop for a while and I have to collect my money.'

'Exactly what is Gordinho's business?' I asked curiously. If Gordinho was expanding his interests in Santos I wanted to hear about it.

'He's bought a place called the Casa Branca. He plans to convert it into a hotel. That's where we're supposed to be meeting tomorrow night.'

'The Casa Branca?'

The name rang a bell but for the moment I couldn't think why.

'Yes, it used to be a restaurant.'

Then I had it. Like Rio de Janeiro, Santos was cramped in area by the steeply rising hills behind the city, restricted to the narrow coast plain, and several blocks of more resistant rock had been left isolated by the centuries of erosion, intruding on the city proper. One of the smaller outcrops necessitated the road tunnel connecting the beach with the main commercial centre but two larger pillars of rock on the Sao Vicente side dominated Santos, rising hundreds of feet above the buildings below. Enterprising businessmen had commissioned minor engineering miracles, driving tortuous, spiral roads up the almost sheer cliff sides and establishing restaurants at the summit. Both of them possessed breathtaking views, with Santos and its wonderful beaches spread out beneath them, but, despite the roads, difficulty of access had hampered trade. To reach the restaurants prospective customers had to face radiator boiling climbs in bottom gear, then brood about the efficiency of their brakes during the meal, afraid to drink because they still had to brave the trip down. One of the restaurants had survived, without doing the business its site and cuisine merited, but the other, the Casa Branca, had folded a couple of years back. Apparently Gordinho now intended to reopen it as a hotel and, provided he lashed out on a chair lift, there was no reason why it shouldn't be a great success.

Now I knew where to find Biddencourt and Gordinho, either at their hotels or the Casa Branca, there were no more questions I wanted to ask Pepe, for the time being anyway. Accordingly, I went through to the bathroom and collected a slab of sticking plaster from the medicine chest. When he saw what I had in my hand Pepe began quaking again.

'I've told you everything you wanted to know,' he quavered. 'You said you'd let me go.'

'That's right,' I agreed, jamming the plaster over his mouth. 'Just as soon as I've dealt with Biddencourt and Gordinho.'

With my prisoner securely strapped to the frame of the bed in the maid's room I took a quick shower before seeing how Rosa was. A damp towel drapped round my waist, I quietly opened my bedroom door and stuck my head into the darkened room. In the dim light coming through the open shutters I could see Rosa curled up in the middle of the double bed, breathing regularly and generally displaying all the manifestations of sleep. Noiselessly I began to shut the door again, only to be interrupted by Rosa's voice.

'Hey,' she said sleepily. 'Where do you think you're sneaking off to? I'm waiting for my pound of flesh.'

CHAPTER XI

AT SOME POINT during the night my subconscious must have started churning over the question of what the hell I intended to do because when I woke up I knew, positively, that I'd lost interest in killing Biddencourt and Gordinho. Certainly the prospect of them dying painfully and unpleasantly didn't bother me at all, I just couldn't think of a good enough reason to shoot them myself. Everything I'd done up to and including the capture of Pepe I could accept without regret but the idea of gunning down the two men in cold blood, which was the way it would have to be done, struck me as completely wrong. Not morally wrong, mind you, just absolutely pointless.

My far from chaste night with Rosa had had a powerful influence on my mental about turn, although there'd been no febrile attack of guilty conscience. What had happened to Lydia hadn't turned me into a hermit. I could still make love to Rosa and enjoy it in the same way I'd made love to her, and other women, when Lydia had been whole and well. The fact I loved Lydia, albeit in my own peculiar fashion, was just that, a basic completely apart from casual copulation. Monogamy had been invented to give every male a fair crack of the whip, not because it was an immutable principle of life, and it was no more reasonable than expecting a man to live on an exclusive diet of fried brussels sprouts.

Nevertheless, once I accepted the proposition that sleeping with Rosa couldn't harm Lydia it was difficult to believe killing Biddencourt and Gordinho would do anything to help her. The damage had been done and it was up to the doctors to help her, not me, and if killing the men responsible for her condition would do nothing to assist Lydia who the hell would it be of value to? Certainly not Otto because he was dead and nothing I did could change this.

Just the same something had to be done, I couldn't turn my back and walk away. The cocaine smuggling wasn't my concern because whatever happened to Biddencourt and Gordinho there would always be people peddling drugs but the knowledge that what had been done to Lydia and Otto could be repeated on other victims made some action essential. And, equally important, there was also the personal factor. From the moment Biddencourt had confronted me at the farmhouse I'd needed to make him realize life just wasn't that easy, that he couldn't do what he'd done by divine right, that he didn't enjoy immunity from the laws governing other men. At first I'd thought killing him was the logical response, now I'd lost a great deal of my enthusiasm.

The problem was to dream up a satisfactory alternative. Rosa had left while I was still asleep, off to work at the Zanzibar, and, once I'd checked Pepe was safe and sound, I spent the rest of the morning reposing in bed, thinking hard with a bottle of Bacardi close to hand. Unless Pepe had been lying, which I couldn't believe, at ten that night I'd have Biddencourt and Gordinho cooped up at the top of a bloody great mountain with one narrow, winding road as their only line of retreat. Given this situation there had to be something my brilliant, incisive brain could come up with.

Calling in the police didn't seem any better an idea than it had the previous day—Gordinho had far too much money for this solution to work—so I was left with Collins. When he'd asked for my assistance I'd given him the brush off, even laid violent hands on him at the football stadium, now I reconsidered my position. Presumably Collins was being paid to smash the cocaine operation and I'd lost all my objections to his earning his money. As soon as Serge phoned in I'd get him to inform Collins about the Casa Branca.

Serge didn't contact me until two in the afternoon, by which time I was on the point of abandoning constructive thought in favour of unrestricted Bacardi drinking. Saved by the telephone bell I wrapped a towel round my waist and went to answer the summons. The Russian sounded distinctly apologetic.

'I've lost him,' he announced. 'I've been waiting for him to come out of the hotel all morning. About half an hour ago I went in to check. The desk clerk said he left really early, before I was back on duty. If I'd had any sense I would have gone in a long while ago.'

To express my annoyance I resorted to basic English, of which I had an excellent command. Somewhat naturally Serge thought my anger was directed at him.

'I'm sorry, Philis,' he said contritely.

'Don't be,' I answered. 'You couldn't be expected to maintain a twenty-four hour watch by yourself. In fact you did well to stay with him for as long as you did. Have you managed to learn anything at the hotel?'

'Your friend is an Englishman named Peter Collins,' Serge told me, relieved that he could be of some use. 'He booked in the day before yesterday for an indefinite stay. According to his passport he's a journalist.'

'Anything else?' I asked, not wanting to disappoint Serge by admitting I'd known most of this before.

'Not really. The desk clerk told me Collins made a phone call to London last night. It was to a man called Pawson.'

Serge's report might provide useful confirmation of what I already knew but he'd still failed in the most vital part of his mission. Collins was on the loose, his whereabouts a mystery, and although I'd exonerated Serge from the blame I was certain I wouldn't have lost him in similar circumstances. If I'd needed to catch up on some beauty sleep I would have slipped the desk clerk a substantial bribe to alert me in the event of Collins departing before I was ready. Serge would probably have done the same if he'd been a man of means but he must have been held back by the knowledge that it was my money he'd be using. Scrupulous honesty sometimes had its drawbacks.

'Collins has to be found by nine o'clock tonight,' I told Serge, keeping my other thoughts to myself. 'I'll phone the Indaia and leave a message for him; you get down to the General Camera and have a scout around there, especially the *Arcadia*. Recruit any help you think you need, expense is no object. When you find Collins tell him where to contact me, say it's urgent.'

'And if I don't manage to find him?'

'In that case ring me at nine,' I instructed him, 'but for God's sake try not to let that happen. If necessary put every tart in the zona on my payroll.'

'OK, I'll do my best.'

On this score I had no doubts, only that seven hours might not provide sufficient time for Serge's best to be good enough.

It was another scorchingly hot day, not that it was ever anything else during a Santos summer, with the lowering, oppressive humidity making conditions ten times worse. Midway through the afternoon came the deceptive, dead calm indicating the onset of a really big storm and I closed the balcony doors, jamming the sofa against them. Then came the wind, rushing in from the sea in a steady eighty mile an hour gale, the torrential rain hard on its heels. Less than half an hour later it was all over, the weather back where it had started even if the streets were flooded. There'd be another big storm within twenty-four hours and perhaps the next one would do something to clear the air instead of just threatening to blow in my balcony windows.

At least the storm did something to break the nervous monotony of waiting for Collins to contact me. Cooking a couple of steaks for Pepe and myself filled in some more time, then I devoted my attention to the second half of the Bacardi bottle, diluting it with Coca Cola although I was too much on edge to be in danger of getting drunk. I carefully nurtured my optimism, telling myself Collins was bound to be found, but nine o'clock came and when the phone rang it was Serge again.

'You haven't found Collins?' I asked.

'I haven't,' Serge admitted. 'I know a lot of places he's been and I know he's looking for you but that's all. What do you want me to do? Keep on looking?'

'Do just that and try a few prayers while you're about it. When you do run him down you can forget about my apartment, I've a message for him instead. Do you know where the Casa Branca is? It's the restaurant at the top of the Sugarloaf or whatever it's called, the one that was closed down.'

'I know where you mean.'

'Good. Well, that's where I'll be, all night if necessary. Tell Collins I should have a couple of people with me that he'd like to meet. They ship coffee on the *Arcadia*, make sure you mention that. OK?'

'I've got it,' Serge said. 'Anything else?'

'Yes, and I'm not so sure Collins will like this part, especially if he's been hiking round Santos all day. Tell him he'll have to walk up to the Casa Branca. If anything should go wrong at my end it wouldn't be wise for him to advertise his arrival.'

For the first time that day I heard Serge laugh.

'I'll tell him,' he promised.

Lighting a Louis XV I walked through to the maid's balcony. It was getting dark and from the tenth floor elevation the lights of the city were below but to see the Casa Branca I had to crane my neck back and look upwards, right up to the summit of the towering hunk of rock erupting from the orderly pattern of houses. Biddencourt and Gordinho were in residence all right. For the first time I could remember lights were blazing from the ex-restaurant and if I'd possessed a pair of binoculars I might have been able to see them. Since Collins had decided to go a-roving I'd have to go up there after all, to hold Biddencourt and Gordinho until he chose to make an appearance. According to Pepe they were already on edge and it might well take only one unforeseen incident to start them running. Like Pepe not arriving on schedule, for example.

Grunting at the exertion, I lifted Pepe from the bed, carted him through into the living-room and threw him on the sofa. When I'd untied him I retreated to an armchair.

'You've just under half an hour to re-start your circulation and get dressed,' I told him. 'Then we're going for a drive.'

'Where to?' Pepe asked suspiciously, grimacing with pain as he rubbed his wrists and ankles.

He was still displaying a lamentable lack of faith, probably thinking I intended to drop him in the harbour.

'The Casa Branca. You've an appointment to keep.'

Although Pepe bent his head and continued rubbing I was convinced I'd glimpsed a glimmer of satisfaction in his eyes. It could just have been relief but I still didn't like it. I far preferred Pepe scared, worrying about his life expectancy, because in this condition he was less likely to try anything cute. Now, although the nervousness remained, the craven cowardice of the previous night had completely disappeared. Try as I might I couldn't think why, or how a trip to the Casa Branca could possibly help him. During the trip my gun wasn't going to move six inches from his spine and I was the last person Biddencourt or Gordinho would expect to see. Nevertheless my uneasiness increased in direct proportion to Pepe's gain in confidence. Laughing at myself I risked leaving Pepe for a minute while I collected the little popgun Melanie had given me. Stuck in my waistband under the sports shirt it pressed uncomfortably against my backbone but at least it was some form of insurance, however poor.

We left for the Casa Branca shortly after half past nine, Pepe driving while I sat behind him. Before we started I'd made my attitude known, promising Pepe that a single slip would be rewarded with a bullet in the head, no matter where we were. Pepe received the message loud and clear and displayed exemplary conduct as we drove towards our objective, working our way across the system of draining canals. When we began the winding climb up to Gordinho's latest acquisition I hunkered down on the floor, keeping the gun pressed against the back of the driving seat. Apparently Gordinho had instructed Pepe to hire a car for the trip and I didn't want anyone up above to realize he had company. As a bonus the manœuvre also effectively prevented me from watching the road, something I was thankful for as it certainly wasn't designed for people with weak nerves. At no point on the ascent was there room for two cars to pass in anything approaching comfort and if a motorist did have the misfortune to meet a vehicle travelling in the opposite direction the alternatives to a head on crash weren't exactly inviting. Pull to the right and the car was heading straight for a rock wall, veer to the left and the prospect was even worse. The drop was sheer only in a few places, otherwise it was a forty-five degree slope of rock and scree with very few chances of halting the car's progress before it was back at sea level. On our little excursion there was no danger of other traffic but the road still wasn't the safest place in the world to be and I was relieved when the DKW spluttered its way on to the acre or so of flat ground at the top.

Light from the Casa Branca flooded the car as we rounded the last corner and I caught a brief glimpse of two men seated on the verandah before I hunched myself even lower. The area of roughly cleared ground intended as a car park was at the far end of the single storied building, in darkness and not overlooked by any windows. Nevertheless this was the danger spot and I hustled Pepe out of the car in double time. It only needed Biddencourt or Gordinho to come to the door as a welcoming committee while I was still stuck in the DKW and my advantage was gone.

Fortunately they evidently didn't consider a menial like Pepe rated moving themselves from their comfortable chairs. With one hand hooked in the Indian's collar and the Nacional jammed against his spine I propelled him up the steps leading to the entrance. Not having more than a sketchy idea of the restaurant's layout the inky darkness inside was a great help.

'Lights,' I breathed in Pepe's ear, not daring to release my grip to hunt for the switch myself.

Pepe located it to the right of the door. We were in a combined lobby and cloak-room just large enough to swing a Manx cat, a rack for coats to one side and a couple of doors leading from it, both closed.

'Lead on,' I whispered, 'and whichever door you choose behave sensibly.'

Without hesitation Pepe plumped for the right hand door and as he opened it I peered over his shoulder, ready to act decisively if Biddencourt or Gordinho had moved from the verandah. They hadn't. The well lit room, once the main dining hall, was deserted, an expanse of dusty boards with chairs and tables stacked the length of one wall. At the far end of the room, a good twenty-five yards away, sliding glass doors connected with the verandah, almost as large as the dining hall itself. From where I stood no one was visible but there was no doubt where they were—Gordinho's voice was clearly audible.

I'd always been told that fortune favoured the brave, now I discovered I hadn't been forgotten either. Reassured, I pushed Pepe through the door and followed him into the dining hall, moving parallel to him as I hugged the left hand wall for concealment. The voice on the verandah stopped when Gordinho heard Pepe walking across the boarded floor.

'You forgot to flash your headlights, Pepe,' Biddencourt called out. 'It's a good job we were expecting you.'

Nervously Pepe glanced across to where I was silently laughing at him, much happier now I knew why Pepe had recovered his confidence. He'd been holding out on me and had neglected to mention the sub-Boy Scout recognition signal which had been arranged. Luckily no one could have taken it too seriously. With my gun I indicated to

Pepe that it was only polite for him to answer when he was spoken to.

'Coming up that blasted road there are a lot more important things to think about than giving signals,' he said sullenly, still walking towards the sliding doors.

Biddencourt laughed, showing he was in a relaxed and jovial mood, and he was still chuckling as I had to abandon the protection of the wall for the last five yards to the verandah. A push between the shoulder blades sent Pepe stumbling through the door and I was right on his heels, relying on speed to prevent Biddencourt and Gordinho from becoming aggressive. There was no need to have worried as they both seemed to be rooted to their chairs, the expressions on their faces suggesting they'd just seen a ghost. If they were fools enough to believe what they read in the newspapers this was a natural reaction.

'Don't bother to rise, gentlemen,' I said pleasantly. 'There's no need to stand on ceremony.'

Even at night the Casa Branca enjoyed a marvellous view, the verandah seemingly suspended hundreds of feet above the city. Far out over the Atlantic there was an electric storm, the diffuse illumination from the sheet lightning brightening the whole horizon. Directly below lay Santos itself, the patchwork of lights dissected by the arrow straight lines of street lamps and bounded on the seaward side by the glittering curve of the esplanade.

Unfortunately I was the only person in a position to appreciate the vista. We were all sitting sociably on the verandah, my three prisoners grouped at one table with their backs to the view and myself a discreet table away, the Nacional pointing loosely in their direction. Biddencourt was busy with his handkerchief, endeavouring to staunch the flow of blood from his nose, and in future he should show considerably more respect when he addressed me. Pepe was back in his scared witless state again, wondering whether I intended to honour my promise to him, but Gordinho seemed completely at ease, relaxed in his chair like a sack of potatoes and idly toying with an ashtray on the table in front of him. The guns I'd taken from Biddencourt and Gordinho lay in the far corner of the verandah, nowhere near enough to be a temptation.

'What are we waiting for?' Gordinho asked, his obsidian eyes unblinkingly levelled at me, just as they had been ever since I'd put in an appearance.

'A good question,' I admitted, deciding there was no reason not to answer him. 'I keep telling myself I ought to shoot you and go home to bed but that would be too easy. Instead we're going to wait for a friend of mine to arrive. What happens then will be entirely up to him.'

Gordinho went back to fiddling with the ashtray, Biddencourt continued dabbing at his nose and Pepe went on shaking. This wasn't particularly stimulating to watch and I hoped Collins arrived before I died of boredom.

'Can you be bought off?' Gordinho asked abruptly. 'You can name your own price.'

'I don't want your money.'

When Gordinho spoke again there was a tinge of regret in his voice.

'I should have had you killed the moment you set foot in Porto Alegre,' he said.

'It would have saved you a lot of trouble,' I agreed, 'but I think Biddencourt made the biggest mistake. I can't understand why he didn't dispose of me at the farmhouse.'

'Nor can I.'

Gordinho flashed a malevolent glance at Biddencourt, who was wholly absorbed with his nose, and at the same instant he threw the ashtray. It was a beautifully executed move. Our conversation had dulled my vigilance, Biddencourt was temporarily the centre of attention and the heavy, glass ashtray had struck my forehead before I realized what was happening. Belying his bulk Gordinho followed up immediately, surging out of his chair and hurling the table after the ashtray as if it weighed nothing. I managed to snap off one wild shot, firing just as the table crashed into my chest, but the bullet did no more than blast a harmless hole in the ceiling. The weight of the table knocked me out of my chair, the gun going loose on the floor, and for the next minute or so everything was chaos.

Pushing the table from my chest I was in a sitting position as Gordinho dived for the gun a couple of feet away from my left hand. To discourage him I brought a foot up into his face and my fingers were actually brushing the butt of the Nacional when Biddencourt jumped me from behind, wrapping his arms round my neck. I let him have my left elbow in the midriff to loosen his hold, then smashed my head back into his face, making the blood spurt between the hands he clasped over his face as he toppled backwards.

Meanwhile Gordinho was still intent on reaching the gun and I hurled myself at him, stretching over his shoulder to knock the Nacional from his grasp. It skittered five or six yards until it lodged harmlessly under a table, temporarily out of play. At once Gordinho started heaving beneath me so I put both hands on the back of his head and slammed his face down on to the concrete floor. This quietened him down considerably, Biddencourt was moaning softly to himself, his hands still over his nose, and I seized the opportunity to scramble to my feet.

All the thrashing around on the floor was getting me nowhere, even if I was well ahead on points, for the struggle had been notable for Pepe's absence. In fact he'd shown far more sense and initiative than either of his bosses and while they'd been wrestling with me on the floor he'd made a beeline for the two guns I'd so nonchalantly tossed into the corner. His first shot as my head came above the level of the tables could have gone anywhere, the second was close enough to tug at the shoulder of my shirt, and I decided not to wait for the third. Instead I took three quick steps, placed one hand on the balustrade of the verandah and vaulted straight over, not giving a damn about the twelve foot drop if this meant I didn't get shot.

Although I landed on my feet I was unable to retain

174

my balance, falling heavily and painfully on to one of the knobs of rock jutting through the sparse, coarse grass. Even so there was no question of staying down for a mandatory eight count, not with one gun already in Pepe's possession and two more lying around for his employers when they felt up to using them. Hugging the wall I scuttled along the front of the verandah, hurled myself round the corner, then began the long run down the back of the building, fumbling the tiny gun Melanie had given me from my pocket, the place I'd transferred it to once I'd mistakenly thought I had the situation under control. My only hope was that I wouldn't have to use it and as far as I was concerned Gordinho and company could do what they liked for the rest of the night. All I wanted was to reach the DKW in safety and head for the hills, praying that no one inside the Casa Branca was sufficiently on the ball to cut me off.

The two shots someone fired after me from the side of the verandah, ricocheting unnervingly from the wall, gave me every incentive to move faster than I'd ever moved before and I reached the end of the building unscathed, the DKW a mere twenty yards away. Nevertheless I didn't make it.

As I rounded the end of the building, the parked cars actually visible to me, someone tried to come round the corner from the opposite direction. The force of the collision bounced me back far enough to see the dim light gleaming on the gun in his right hand. Instinctively, operating purely at reflex level, my left hand swept up, banging his wrist against the sharp edge of the building, and simultaneously, at a range of little over a yard, I fired both bullets from the gun Melanie had given me into his stomach.

Only as he folded forward with a coughing gurgle did my brain register any image other than the one of the gun in his hand, then two impressions clicked up at the same time. Pepe would have had to be an Olympic sprint champion to run the whole length of the restaurant, down the steps and along the end of the building in time to bump into me at the corner and, far more important, the man I'd just shot wasn't Pepe in any case. Nor was he Biddencourt or Gordinho.

Collins had eventually bumped into Serge or received the message I'd left for him at the Indaia and come post haste to the Casa Branca where I'd belly shot him on arrival. Cursing fluently under my breath I dropped the useless gun and caught him under the armpits, not so much aghast at what I'd done to Collins—it was odds of thousands to one against me hitting anything vital with Melanie's popgun—as appalled at the thought of gunning down my own reinforcements.

Collins didn't stay tenderly cradled in my arms for very long. As soon as I heard someone cautiously pulling at the handle of the door at the head of the steps some ten yards away, the one I'd gone in with Pepe, I dumped him unceremoniously on the ground. With Collins's gun in my hand, a hefty, well balanced revolver which gave me a hell of a sight more confidence than the puny thing I'd had before, I squatted against the wall, waiting for whoever it was to show himself. Not that I'd changed my mind about the getaway in the DKW, it was just I couldn't afford to leave with this threat to my rear.

All the advantages were on my side. I had my night vision and knew exactly where the opposition would have to show themselves whereas they could have no more than a general idea of my position. Patiently I waited, the revolver held in both hands, my elbows braced against my knees, aiming at the ever widening gap of the inwards opening door. Whoever was coming out was being ultra-cautious. The noise I'd made shooting Collins would have warned the people inside that I was armed, although they must have wondered what on earth I'd been shooting at, and appropriate precautions were being taken. The door was fully opened, a dark rectangle against the grey of the wall, and still I could see nobody. On either side of the steps leading up to the entrance there was a three foot wall and if anyone had come outside he was being careful to stay behind cover. Just the same he had to expose himself sometime and until then I had nowhere else to go. My main worry was the second door, the one I'd run past in my retreat from the verandah, but so far there was no indication of any threat from this direction.

On the first occasion Pepe stuck his head above the wall it only stayed there long enough for me to recognise him and I held my fire because the whole object of this little exercise was for Pepe to see if anyone felt inclined to take potshots at him. Being of a nervous disposition he tried the stratagem a second time and again I declined to waste a bullet, preferring to wait for a stationary target.

The third time was for real, Pepe had stopped messing around and was intent on a proper survey. Before I fired I lined up carefully, not rushing myself because he was still only offering me his head to aim at. The revolver must have thrown a trifle low, chipping off a splinter of stone from the top of the wall, but not so much that this made any difference. The bullet, ricocheting upwards into his face at an angle, lifted him up to his full height, his outstretched arms silhouetted against the dark grey of the sky behind, before he folded, the upper half of his body draped limply over the wall. As I watched Pepe began to slide forward, slowly at first, then faster as his centre of gravity shifted, until his body dropped from its precarious perch, landing in a lifeless heap no more than six yards from where I crouched.

I allowed thirty seconds for any reactions from the other two men in the Casa Branca. There were none and I decided to make my try for the DKW, preferring a car I knew to the superior performance of the Mercedes parked beside it, the vehicle belonging to Biddencourt and Gordinho. This meant I'd risk exposing myself to anyone in the doorway Pepe had come through but at least I'd have Collins on my back as some form of shield. He was conscious and had been ever since I'd shot him. While I'd been waiting for a shot at Pepe he'd obligingly held his breath, now it was coming between his clenched teeth in little, sobbing moans.

'Do you think you can walk?' I whispered, heaving him into a sitting position against the wall. 'I'm going to try to get you to one of the cars.'

For a man with stomach wounds Collins shook his head with surprising vehemence.

'I'm not leaving,' he said hoarsely, every word an effort. 'Now we've started we've got to deal with the others as well.'

'Speak for yourself,' I told him. 'With you or without you I'm going.'

'Take a step towards the cars and I'll raise blue, bloody murder,' he threatened. 'That's a promise.'

This was a ridiculous remark to make, the obvious answer being to belt him hard on the head, and for a moment I was seriously tempted. My hostility to Biddencourt and Gordinho wasn't, by itself, sufficient reason for me to risk being killed but the two lead pellets I'd fired into Collins's gut did mean I had a certain responsibility for him. Otto and Reece had already been killed, Lydia was on my conscience and I couldn't just abandon Collins. This gave me one good reason for doing my damnedest to kill Gordinho and Biddencourt.

The second reason had suddenly occurred to me quite independently. Assuming I reached the DKW there would be at least one hundred metres to cover when the car would be completely exposed to anyone inside the Casa Branca. Bullets from one side and a drop of several hundred feet on the other seemed more than adequate motives for postponing my thoughts of a drive.

'You're right,' I whispered to Collins, sneering at myself in the darkness. 'We mustn't let the bastards escape. Just hang on for a second. I'll be right back.'

Cautiously I crawled over to Pepe's corpse and, after a few seconds' scrabbling around, found the gun, still clutched tightly in his hand. To pry it loose I had to break a couple of fingers, something I didn't particularly enjoy doing although Pepe didn't raise any objections, and then I made my way back to Collins. The lights had been doused inside the building, otherwise there were no signs of activity.

'How do you feel?' I asked as I handed over the gun.

'I'll survive so long as I don't have to do any running around.'

Although he was obviously in pain I tended to agree with him. It would have taken a very lucky shot to kill him and his lucidity and alertness certainly didn't indicate a mortal wound.

'You won't even have to move from here,' I assured him. 'Just sit here and shoot anyone who comes out of that door or tries to use either of the cars. There are two men inside, both armed, and they probably think I'm alone out here. They have to leave the building some time and when they do there's only one other exit, the door I'll be covering. If they should decide to slip through one of the windows or over the verandah and then hoof it down the mountain we've lost them. Otherwise we're sitting pretty. OK?'

'You're over-simplifying,' Collins answered, 'but offhand I can't think of anything better. There is one point though —try to remember that the longer we stay here the more blood I lose.'

Ignoring this sneak attack on my conscience I left Collins at his post. Of course he could think of a better plan—from his point of view, that is. He wanted me to go inside to flush the opposition out, something I'd absolutely no intention of attempting. It was one thing to be prepared to do my best to see Collins to safety, quite another to be fool enough to risk sticking my head inside the Casa Branca. Either we collared Biddencourt and Gordinho when they decided to break from cover or we didn't catch them at all.

For twenty minutes I crouched beside the steps leading to the second entrance, all my senses straining to pick up

179

sounds of activity inside, and when I did hear something I refused to credit the evidence of my ears, putting it down to imagination. Another slithering sound from above showed my ears hadn't been deceiving me, that there really was someone on the roof.

Instinctively I huddled deeper into the shadow of the steps, doing my best to compress myself into an indistinct shape about two centimetres square. After sixty seconds' existence as a still life I was convinced of two things. The man on the roof was moving so quietly he could only be Biddencourt—it was difficult enough to visualize Gordinho hauling himself up on to the roof, downright impossible to imagine him trying to crawl around on his protuberant stomach. Furthermore Biddencourt wasn't my problem, he was Collins's. Although there weren't too many sounds to trace his progress by there were enough to tell me he was moving away from me, towards the car park. When he finally stopped he was somewhere above the main entrance, a fact which made me very glad I was me and not Peter Collins.

I was considering what I could do to help when the problem was resolved for me. Collins must have had a lot more practice than Biddencourt at getting from place to place without making a noise because, even with a couple of bullets in him, I wouldn't have realized he was easing himself round the corner towards me unless I'd happened to be looking in that direction.

The penny dropped then and I stopped trying to blend in with the scenery, going up the steps as fast as caution allowed. It was a pleasant surprise to discover the hinges of the door didn't squeak but once inside I had to waste valuable time while I tried to spot the obstacles in my path. The room had once been a kitchen and was littered with all manner of cooking equipment, meaning that in the near pitch darkness I had to work my way round the periphery of the room, past cupboards, draining boards and a sink, until I reached the exit I'd been looking for.

Some thoughtful soul had left this door open and it

led to a corridor which seemed to run in the direction I wanted. My mouth dry, pulse rate up in the low thousands, I forced myself forward, my shoulder brushing the right hand wall and an arm held out in front of me to give warning of what I was likely to bump into. There was nothing like stark, unadulterated fear to heighten my sensitivity and if anyone had dropped a pin within half a mile of me I would probably have jumped out of my skin. Philis reasoning power told me Gordinho should be crouching behind the same wall Pepe had used, plucking up his courage to walk the few paces to the car while Biddencourt covered him from the roof. Unfortunately this selfsame reasoning power had let me down so often in the past it wasn't hard to visualize myself walking blind on to the end of Gordinho's gun.

Instead my lead hand brushed against wood and I untensed my stomach muscles. I'd taken twelve shuffling steps from the kitchen so the door should be one of those leading to the lobby. Treating the handle as though depressing it too fast would bring the ceiling down on my head I inched the door open a fraction prior to hooking an eyebrow round the edge. I was too late and, typically, Gordinho was doing things in style. He wasn't the man to demean himself by skulking in the shadows and there was no attempt at concealment, his familiar, purposeful tread as he strolled to the cars clearly audible where I stood.

More relaxed now I knew where everyone was I crossed the lobby, reaching the door in time to watch Gordinho skirt the DKW on his way to the Mercedes.

There was nothing of Gordinho's aplomb about Biddencourt. He was still acutely aware of my possible presence in the vicinity and it took him several minutes to scramble down from the roof and make his way through the building to where I was waiting. He'd descended two of the steps before I came out from behind the door.

'Stand still and drop your gun,' I said softly, giving him a chance he didn't deserve.

Biddencourt must have been as tense as I'd been when I entered the building, starting to turn before I'd finished speaking and, without hesitation, firing back into the open doorway. I allowed him two shots, both bullets whining harmlessly over my head as I lay comfortably on the floor, then I put a bullet through his chest. We were so close he seemed to fly backwards, the hammerblow lifting him clear of the steps and hurling him a good five yards through the air to land on his back on the rough ground of the car park.

In the few seconds it had taken Biddencourt to die both men outside had gone into action. At the sound of the first shot Gordinho had started the Mercedes and Collins had opened up from his corner, his carefully spaced shots thunking into the bodywork of the car. I gave him four hits out of four but he missed both Gordinho and the petrol tank because the Mercedes was out of the car park and disappearing down the road before I could make any contribution.

It was the glaring injustice which started me running down the steps. Gordinho was the top man, the person ultimately responsible for the disruption of my peaceful life in Brazil, and it was unthinkable that he should be the only one to escape. As I ran across the car park Collins shouted something after me but I ignored him, the same way I ignored the DKW, heading instead in a direction diametrically opposed to the one Gordinho had taken.

Although I was prepared for the slope I didn't manage to stay on my feet. The ground seemed to drop away from me and instead of running I was sliding on the seat of my pants, my feet making a bow wave in the scree. Thirty feet or so of this and a rocky outcrop brought me to a painful halt. At the second attempt I managed six steps, then I was down again, rolling this time until the next rock came along.

It was a rut I didn't think I'd ever escape—fall, slide, hit a rock, up on my feet, fall again. Luckily I was on my feet when I cut the road for the first time, the only reason

I didn't break my neck. My second step after bouncing off yet another rock and I was space walking, floating above the lights of the city until, ten feet down, I hit the tarmac, doing a paratroop roll to save my legs. Before it occurred to me to give up I was sliding feet first again and once the pattern was re-established I had no real choice in the matter. At least the gaps in the trail of skin I was leaving behind me were growing longer as I adjusted to the routine, a kind of skiing without skis which increased my speed while cutting down on the falls. There were even small trees to break my fall at the next cliff, growing out of the cracks in the rock face, and the branches whipping back across my face were amply compensated for by my feather bed landing, a drop of no more than six feet to the road from where I hung on to one of the sturdier trees.

And there was the satisfaction of discovering I was ahead of Gordinho. My unconventional route hadn't been more than two hundred yards in a straight line, on the road it would have been well over half a mile with speed right out of the question and Gordinho was approaching the bend fifty yards uphill from where I'd landed. I knelt on one knee in the middle of the road, flexing the bruised and grazed knuckles of my right hand while I watched the headlights of the Mercedes, at first cutting twin paths in the dark void above the city, gradually swinging inwards as Gordinho slowed down into the bend until they merged into one dazzling, white beam as the car finally negotiated the corner.

On seeing the obstruction in his path Gordinho slowed momentarily, almost immediately stamping on the accelerator as he recognized it for what it was, leaping the Mercedes towards me in a surge of power. Grimly I willed myself to remain where I was, the revolver clutched in both hands and aimed above the headlights on the driver's side. At thirty yards my nerve broke and I cut loose, the gun bucking wildly in my hands as I frantically squeezed the trigger until, mercifully, the hammer dropped on an empty chamber and I could throw myself to the left, out of the path of the approaching juggernaut. My evasive action wasn't a moment too soon. The wheels passed so close that small stones hurled up by them splattered my face and the slipstream felt like a small hurricane, threatening to rip the shirt from my back, but I was untouched and the car kept on its course. There was no wobbling, no yawing, absolutely nothing to show my bullets had done any damage —except that there was no slackening of speed as the Mercedes went into the next corner.

The offside wing ploughed into the rock face with a grinding, metal-buckling crash, turning the car on to its roof without losing forward momentum. Upside down and at thirty miles an hour the Mercedes became a flying hearse, sailing yards through the air before there was a second scream of tortured metal striking rocks. On this first bounce the petrol tank exploded, shooting flames high in the air, and the car was transformed into a fireball rolling down the mountainside with undiminished speed, its progress easy to follow even after the car itself was out of my sight.

It was my own personally produced cataclysm and the sight must have thrown me into shock. I should have been moving, doing something to get Collins and myself off that blasted mountain, but I just stood helplessly at the side of the road, gazing at the glow from the fiercely burning wreckage. Only the sound of a second car descending from the Casa Branca snapped me back to reality. Anxiously I swung round, willing Collins to make it. It was madness for him even to think of driving, especially on that road, but at least he was giving us a chance to leave the vicinity before anyone thought of visiting the Casa Branca to check the starting point of the wrecked Mercedes.

The DKW was moving at little more than walking pace, mainly because he sensibly wasn't showing any lights, and it seemed like hours before he pulled up beside me, opening the driver's door and sliding across into the passenger seat himself. He sat hunched there, both hands

clutching his stomach, while I hastily settled myself behind the wheel. Collins must have been on the far side of the
mountain when the Mercedes began its spectacular descent
for he was staring fixedly at the flames, an expression of
awe on his face.

'I knew I could trust you to be discreet,' he said weakly
as I released the hand brake.

EPILOGUE

GREGSON WAS as big as he was ugly and he was very, very
ugly. Stripped to the skin, he stood six feet four inches and
weighed over seventeen stone; wrapped up in a duffle coat
and scarf against the bitter cold of a grey Liverpool dawn he
seemed twice the size. As Philis walked away from the
ship Gregson stepped in front of him, placing one enormous
hand flat on his chest and pushing him back a couple of
paces.

'Someone wants to see you.'

Gregson made no effort to be civil, doing nothing to
make his approach anything but unpleasant. For a second he
thought Philis was going to take a swing at him, then the
other man relaxed. Two inches shorter than Gregson, he
stood there in his thin, tropical suit, a battered suitcase in
his right hand.

'Get stuffed,' Philis answered, a slight smile on his face. 'I
can't think of anyone you're likely to know who I'd want
to meet.'

Philis had started forward again, intending to skirt
Gregson who hadn't moved from his path. Gregson responded by grabbing Philis's free arm with both hands,
twisting it behind his back and pushing the wrist so high
between his shoulder-blades that Philis grunted with pain.

'Let's go,' Gregson ordered, his tone harsh.

The muscles beneath Gregson's hands tensed, preparing
for the violent action which would cost Philis a broken
arm, but the resistance was only momentary, ceasing when
Philis sensed the strength of the man holding him.

'For Christ's sake,' he protested. 'You're hurting me.
My arm isn't supposed to bend that way.'

In reply Gregson hauled his arm a couple of inches
higher, provoking another grunt, and propelled his prisoner
towards the Bentley which was parked a hundred yards

away. He hadn't expected it to be so easy. Pawson had warned him to be ready for fireworks but handling Philis had proved to be like taking sweets from a baby.

On this, his first showing, Philis was a grave disappointment to Pawson. From the photographs he'd been prepared for his physical characteristics—the muscular, athletic build, his normal, good-humoured expression, the unruly mop of black hair. What he had been totally unprepared for was the meekness with which he'd allowed himself to be manhandled by the oafish Gregson.

Admittedly, not many people could be expected to come out on top in a rough and tumble with Gregson, his brute strength being nature's compensation for his lack of brain, but both Reece and Collins had praised Philis to the skies, going into raptures about his resource and adaptability. The impression they, and Peters, had given was of a natural, someone definitely not to be trifled with, yet trifle with him was exactly what Gregson had just done. There hadn't been the slightest display of aggression or defiance and, watching Philis squirm ineffectually in Gregson's implacable grip, Pawson began to suspect Reece and Collins had merely been attempting to divert attention from their own deficiencies.

'Will you tell your tame gorilla to let go of my arm?' Philis pleaded when he reached the car. 'I may need it again.'

Through the rolled down window of the Bentley Pawson examined his pain-racked face. He was frightened and hurt, a tough who had met someone just a little too big and strong for him. Definitely not SR(2) material, only a loose end to be tidied up.

'All right, Gregson,' Pawson said, irritated by the wasted journey to Liverpool. He'd had a lot of plans for Philis. 'Give him his arm back.'

Gregson released his hold, smiling contemptuously. He was disappointed as well—he'd been looking forward to a work-out with no holds barred.

'He's quite strong for a growing lad,' Philis commented.

The bravado failed to ring true, the wince as Philis flexed his bruised arm belying the flip tone.

Seconds later Pawson had to revise his opinion. There was no warning, the decision to act and its implementation absolutely simultaneous. The heavy suitcase in Philis's right hand swung up between Gregson's legs with sickening force, the blade of his left burying itself in Gregson's throat a fraction of a second later. Pawson's despondency began to disperse, vanishing completely when Philis put the boot in, a measured kick behind the ear, after which Gregson ceased his agonized writhing on the ground.

'Satisfied?' Philis asked with a grin. 'I thought you'd prefer a grandstand seat, rather than have me rough him up in the middle distance.'

Pawson laughed, amused by the arrogance of the man and thinking it should prove even more amusing to take him down a peg or two. Unasked, Philis walked round the bonnet of the car and slid into the front seat beside Pawson, throwing his suitcase into the back.

'I take it you're Pawson.'

This was more a statement than a question.

'That is correct.'

Philis pulled out a cigarette and lit it, not offering one to Pawson. He seemed completely at his ease.

'You should be the one lying out there,' he said. 'Not Grierson or whatever his name is. You're lucky I'm not the kind of person to bear a grudge.'

'You mean the girl?'

'Chiefly, yes.'

'I'm sorry about what happened to her.' Pawson's regret was genuine. 'I've arranged for her to have the best possible treatment.'

Philis smiled cynically but said nothing. Outside Gregson was beginning to groan but not loudly enough to compete with the tooting of the tugs on the river.

Pawson and Philis were alone in the hotel suite, a modern,

brightly decorated room halfway up the tower of concrete and glass, both of them comfortably seated with a whisky near to hand.

'What do you plan to do now you're back in England?' Pawson asked.

He already knew the answer. Philis was going to work for SR(2), whether this figured in his present plans or not.

'I was thinking of a career in journalism,' Philis answered blandly.

Although he remained outwardly calm Pawson was bubbling with mirth inside. The nerve of the cocky upstart, he was thinking, the absolute bloody neck to consider blackmailing him, Pawson. The more he saw of Philis the more he admired his style, not that this would save him from being put firmly in his place.

'Have you had any experience?' Pawson only just managed to keep a straight face as he spoke. 'It's a difficult profession to break into.'

'It shouldn't be too much of a problem. I've quite a good story to sell.'

Philis was mocking him now, the smile softening his features and making him look almost boyish.

'You weren't thinking of publishing your Brazilian memoirs by any chance?' Pawson queried, finding it increasingly difficult to maintain his sober exterior.

'How ever did you guess?' The guileless expression on Philis's face was a minor classic.

Thoughtfully Pawson pushed himself from his armchair and walked across to the sideboard to replenish his glass, an action which was entirely for Philis's benefit. In reality it was no more than an excuse for Pawson to turn away for a minute in order to release the smile he could bottle up no longer.

'I very much doubt whether the English press would dare to publish it,' he said from the sideboard, his back still turned. 'In fact I can guarantee they wouldn't.'

'You're probably right,' Philis admitted, unabashed, 'but I've heard they have a far more liberal attitude on the continent. Magazines like *Der Spiegel*, for example.'

'I suppose I couldn't persuade you to change your mind?'

'You might be able to,' Philis admitted. 'Of course, it would rather depend on what you're prepared to offer.'

His glass filled to his satisfaction, Pawson returned to his armchair, no longer bothering to conceal his amusement.

'I'll offer you a passport,' he said once he was seated, 'and a job with SR(2). As a bonus I'll forget the money we had to pay that Brazilian police inspector.'

'A passport?'

Philis was visibly taken aback.

'Yes, the immigration people are very strict about them. I know you're British, you know you're British, but for all Customs know you could be a white Pakistani. Once they discovered you didn't have a genuine passport, only that forged affair Collins arranged for you, they'd ship you straight back to Brazil. You might find it quite a problem to persuade the Rio Grande police to return the documents they're looking after for you.'

Philis took it remarkably well, far better than Pawson could have expected, and there was no rancour in his laugh.

'You bastard,' he said. 'Do you mind if I call you sir?'

F   cop.2

Perry
    The fall guy